ASK the PARROT

By Richard Stark

The Hunter
The Man with the Getaway Face
The Outfit
The Mourner
The Score
The Jugger
The Seventh
The Handle
The Damsel
The Rare Coin Score
The Green Eagle Score
The Dame
The Black Ice Score
The Sour Lemon Score
Deadly Edge
The Blackbird
Slayground
Lemons Never Lie
Plunder Squad
Butcher's Moon
Comeback
Backflash
Flashfire
Firebreak
Breakout
Nobody Runs Forever

ASK the PARROT

RICHARD STARK

Quercus

First published in Great Britain in 2007 by

Quercus
21 Bloomsbury Square
London
WC1A 2NS

A CIP catalogue reference for this book is available from the British Library

ISBN (HB) 1 84724 039 9
(978 1 84724 039 2)
ISBN (TPB) 1 84724 040 2
(978 1 84724 040 8)

10 9 8 7 6 5 4 3 2 1

Typeset by e-type, Liverpool
Printed and bound in Great Britain by
Clays Ltd, St Ives plc.

part one

one

When the helicopter swept northward and lifted out of sight over the top of the hill, Parker stepped away from the tree he'd waited beside and continued his climb. Whatever was on the other side of this hill had to be better than the dogs baying down there at the foot of the slope behind him, running around, straining at their leashes, finding his scent, starting up. He couldn't see the bottom of the hill any more, the police cars congregated around his former Dodge rental in the diner parking lot, but he didn't need to. The excited yelp of the dogs was enough.

How tall was this hill? Parker wasn't dressed for uphill hiking, out in the midday October air; his street shoes skidded on leaves, his jacket bunched when he pulled himself up from tree trunk to tree trunk. But he still had to keep ahead of the dogs and hope to find something or somewhere useful when he finally started down the other side.

How much farther to the top? He paused, holding the rough bark of a tree, and looked up, and fifteen feet above him through the scattered thin trunks of this second-growth woods there stood a man. The afternoon sun was to Parker's left, the sky beyond the man a pale October ash, the man himself only a silhouette. With a rifle.

Not a cop. Not with a group. A man standing, looking down toward Parker, hearing the same hounds Parker heard, holding the rifle easy at a slant across his front, pointed up and to the side. Parker looked down again, chose the next tree trunk, pulled himself up.

It was another three or four minutes before he drew level with the man, who stepped back a pace and said, "That's good. Right there's good."

"I have to keep moving," Parker said, but he stopped, wishing these shoes gave better traction on dead leaves.

The man said, "You one of those robbers I've been hearing about on the TV? Took all a bank's money, over in Massachusetts?"

Parker said nothing. If the rifle moved, he would have to meet it.

The man watched him, and for a few seconds they only considered one another. The man was about fifty, in a red leather hunting jacket with many pockets, faded blue jeans, and black boots. His eyes were shielded by a billed red and black flannel cap. Beside him on the ground was a gray canvas sack, partly full, with brown leather handles.

Seen up close, there was a tension in the man that seemed to be a part of him, not something caused by running into a fugitive in the woods. His hands were clenched on the rifle, and his eyes were bitter, as though something had harmed him at some point and he was determined not to let it happen again.

Then he shook his head and made a downturned mouth, impatient with the silence. "The reason I ask," he said, "when I saw you coming up, and heard the dogs, I thought if you are one of the robbers, I want to talk to you." He shrugged, a pessimist to his boots, and said, "If you're not, you can stay here and pat the dogs."

"I don't have it on me," Parker said.

Surprised, the man said, "Well, no, you couldn't. It was about a truckload of cash, wasn't it?"

"Something like that."

The man looked downhill. The dogs couldn't be seen yet, but they could be heard, increasingly frantic and increasingly excited, held back by their handlers' lesser agility on the hill. "This could be your lucky day," he said, "and mine, too." Another sour face. "I could use one." Stooping to pick up his canvas sack, he said, "I'm hunting for the pot, that's what I'm doing. I have a car back here."

Parker followed him the short climb to the crest, where the trees were thinner but within a cluster of them a black Ford SUV was parked on a barely visible dirt road. "Old logging road," the man said, and opened the back cargo door of the SUV to put the rifle and sack inside. "I'd like it if you'd sit up front."

"Sure."

Parker got into the front passenger seat as the man came around the other side to get behind the wheel. The key was already in the ignition. He started the car and drove them at an angle down the wooded north slope, the road usually visible only because it was free of trees.

Driving, eyes on the dirt lane meandering downslope ahead of them, the man said, "I'm Tom Lindahl. You should give me something to call you."

"Ed," Parker decided.

"Do you have any weapons on you, Ed?"

"No."

"There's police roadblocks all around here."

"I know that."

"What I mean is, if you think you can jump me and steal my car, you wouldn't last more than ten minutes."

Parker said, "Can you get around the roadblocks?"

"It's only a few miles to my place," Lindahl said. "We won't run into anybody. I know these roads."

"Good."

Parker looked past Lindahl's sour face, downslope to the left, and through the trees now he could just see a road, two-lane blacktop, below them and running parallel to them. A red pickup truck went by down there, the opposite way, uphill. Parker said, "Can they see us from the road, up in here?"

"Doesn't matter."

"They'll get to the top in a few minutes, with the dogs," Parker said. "They'll see this road, they'll figure I'm in a car."

"Soon we'll be home," Lindahl said, and unexpectedly laughed, a rusty sound as though he didn't do much laughing. "You're the reason I came out," he said.

"Oh, yeah?"

"The TV's full of the robbery, all that money gone, I couldn't stand it any more. Those guys don't get slapped around, I thought. Those guys aren't afraid of their own shadow, they go out and do what has to be done. I got so mad at myself – I'll tell you right now, I'm a coward – I just had to come out with the gun awhile. Those two rabbits back there, I can use them, God knows, but I didn't really need them just yet. It was you brought me out."

Parker watched his profile. Now that he was talking, Lindahl seemed just a little less bitter. Whatever was bothering him, it must make it worse to hold it in.

Lindahl gave him a quick glance, his expression now almost merry. "And here you are," he said. "And up close, I got to tell you, you don't look like that much of a world-beater."

He steered left, down a steep slope, and the logging road met the blacktop.

two

The name on the town sign was Pooley, and it wasn't much of a place. One minor intersection was controlled by a light blinking amber in two directions, red in the other two. A gas station stood on the corner there, along with a shut-down bank branch, a shut-down bar, and a shut-down sporting goods store. Twenty houses or so were strung along the two narrow roads of the town, three or four of them boarded up, most of the rest dilapidated. An old man slept in a rocker on a porch, and an old woman a few doors down knelt at her front-lawn garden.

Lindahl drove straight through the intersection, then three houses later turned to the right into a gravel driveway next to one of the boarded-up houses. Behind the house, at the rear of the property, a three-car brown clapboard garage had been converted to housing, and that was where Lindahl stopped.

"You go on in," he said. "It isn't locked. I'll take care of my rabbits."

Parker got out of the Ford and walked over to what had originally been the middle garage door, now crudely converted to a front door next to a double-hung window covered on the inside by a venetian blind.

He pushed open this door and stepped into a dim interior, where the smell, not strong, was cavelike, old dirt combined with some kind of animal scent. Then he saw the parrot, in a large cage on top of the television set. The parrot saw him, too, turning his green head to the side to do it, but didn't speak, only made a small gurgling sound and briefly marched in place on its bar. The newspaper in the bottom of its cage was not new.

The rest of the living room was normal but seedy, with old furniture not cared for. The television set was on, sound off, showing an antacid commercial.

Lindahl's anger was money-based. He wasn't supposed to be needy, living like this, shooting rabbits to feed himself. Hearing about a big-scale robbery had made him angrier and depressed and self-hating; which meant there was something he should have done about the money he felt was rightfully his, but he hadn't done it. And now he thought that talking with a bank robber would help.

Parker spent the next five minutes lightly tossing the place: living room, bedroom, bath, kitchen, utility room with oil furnace. Three more rifles were locked to a wall rack in the bedroom, but there were no pistols. Lindahl lived here alone and didn't seem to have much correspondence with anybody. He had a checking account with $273 in it, and wrote checks only for standard items like phone and electricity, plus ATM withdrawals for cash. A $1,756 deposit every month was labeled "dis"; disability?

Lindahl would tell him why he'd rather talk to a bank robber than turn him in. Whatever the reason, right now Parker needed it. The only identification he carried was no good any more, now that the police had the car he'd rented with it. For the next couple of days, in this part of the world, it would be impossible to travel anywhere, even by foot, without having to show ID every once in a while.

When Lindahl walked in, carrying his rifle and two white plastic bags, Parker was in the living room, seated on the chair that didn't face the television set, leafing through yesterday's local blat. From the headlines, it seemed to be all small towns around here, no cities.

Parker looked up at the door opening, and Lindahl said, "I'll just take care of this and wash my hands," and went on through to the kitchen. Parker heard the water run, and then Lindahl came back, now carrying only the rifle, loose in one hand. "One more thing," he said, and went into the bedroom, and Parker heard the click as the rifle was locked into its place on the wall.

Now at last Lindahl came out to the living room and sat down on the left side of the sofa. "I've been trying to think how to tell you," he said. "I'm not used to talking to people any more."

He stopped and looked over at Parker, as though waiting for a response, but Parker said nothing. So Lindahl made his sour chuckle and said, "I guess you're the same."

"You have something to tell me."

"I'm a whistle-blower," Lindahl said, as though he'd been planning some much longer way to say it. "My wife told me not to do it, she said I'd lose everything including her, and she was right. But I'm bullheaded."

"Where did you blow this whistle?"

"I worked for twenty-two years at a racetrack down toward Syracuse," Lindahl said, "named Gro-More. It was named after a farm feed company went bankrupt forty years ago. They never changed the name."

"You blew a whistle."

"I was a manager, I was in charge of infrastructure, the upkeep of the buildings, the stands, the track. Hired people, contracted out. I was nothing to do with money."

"So whatever this is," Parker said, "you shouldn't have known about it."

"I didn't have to know about it." Lindahl shook his head, explaining himself. "What we had was a clean track," he said. "The people working there, we were all happy to be at a clean track. There's a thousand ways for a track to be dirty, but only one way to be clean, so when I found out what they were doing with the money, it just hurt me. It was like doing something dirty to a member of my own family."

The strain of getting his point across was deepening the lines in his face. He broke off, made erasing gestures, and said, "I need a beer. I can't tell this without a beer." Rising, he said, "You want one?"

"No, but you go ahead."

Lindahl did, and when he was seated again, he said, "What they were doing, they were hiding illegal campaign contributions to state politicians, running them through the track. Laundering them, you might say."

Parker said, "How would that work?"

"A fella goes to the track, he bets a thousand dollars on a long shot on every race, he drops eight thousand that day. Just that day. That money stays in the system, because he did it with credit cards, but a lot of little penny ante bets from other people disappear. Bets made with cash. So the guy didn't give the politician the eight thousand, he just lost it at the track, but a little later it shows up in a politician's pocket."

"The horses gave it to him."

"That's about it," Lindahl agreed. "When I found out about it, I was just stunned. We never had dope at the track, we never had fixed races, we never had ringers, we never had the mob, and now this. I talked to one of the execs, he didn't see the problem. They're just helping out some friends, nobody from the track is making any money off it. This is just trying to get around some of those stupid pain-in-the-ass regulations from Washington."

"Makes it sound good," Parker said.

"But it isn't good." Lindahl swigged beer. "This is just corruption everywhere you look, the politicians, the track, the whole idea of sports. I talked it over with my wife, we talked about it for months, she told me it was none of my business, I'd lose my job, I'd lose everything. We never had a lot of money, she said if I threw our life away she wouldn't stick around. But I couldn't help it, I finally went to the state police."

"You wear a wire?"

"Yes, I did." Lindahl looked agonized. "That's the part I really regret," he said. "If I just said look, this is going on, then I'm just the guy who saw it is all. But the prosecutors leaned on me, they got me to help them make their case. And then, at the end, the politics was just too strong for them, it all got swept under the carpet, and nothing happened to anybody but me."

"You knew that was going to happen."

"I suppose I did," Lindahl said, and drank some more of his beer. "They talked me into it, but I suppose I talked myself into it, too. Thinking it was best for the track, can you believe that? Not best for me, best for some goddam racetrack named after cow feed, I should have my head examined."

"Too late," Parker said.

Lindahl sighed. "Yes, it is," he said. "Everybody told me don't worry, there's whistle-blower laws, they can't touch you." He gestured with the beer bottle, indicating the room. "You see where I am. My wife was true to her word, she went off with her widowed sister. I haven't had a job for four years. I get a little disability from when a horse rolled over me, years ago, I don't even limp any more, but I'm the wrong age and the wrong background and in the wrong part of the country to find anybody to hire me to do anything. Even flipping burgers, they don't want somebody my age."

"No, they don't," Parker said. "So you've been kicking yourself that you didn't get even. Because you think you could get even. How?"

"I ran those buildings for years," Lindahl said. "I've still got up-to-date keys for every door out there. I still go out every once in a while, when there isn't any meet going on, when it's shut down like a museum, and I just walk around it. Every once in a while, if I find a door with a new key, I borrow a spare from the rack and make a copy for myself."

"You can get in and out."

"I can not only get in and out," Lindahl said, "I know where to get in and out. I know where the money goes, and where the money waits, and where the money's loaded up for the bank, and where the money's stored till the armored car gets there. I know where everything is and how to get to everything. During a meet, the place is guarded 24/7, but I know how to slide a truck in there, three in the morning, no one the wiser. I know how to get in, and then I know how to carry a heavy weight out."

Lindahl had already carried a heavy weight out of that place, but that wasn't what he meant. Parker said, "So once they cost you your wife and your job, you decided to rip them off, get a new stake, go away and retire in comfort."

"That's right," Lindahl said. "I've been thinking about nothing else for four years."

"Why didn't you do it?"

"Because I'm a useless spineless coward," Lindahl said, and finished his beer.

three

"Or it could be," Parker said, "you're just not that dumb."

Lindahl frowned at him. "In what way?"

"You go in there some night," Parker said, "three in the morning with your truck and your keys and your inside knowledge, and you load the truck up with their cash, and when they find the cash gone next morning, nothing broken into, what's the first thing they say? They say, 'Do we have a disgruntled ex-employee around here?' "

"Oh, I know that," Lindahl said, and laughed at himself, shaking his head. "That was a part of the whole idea. It wasn't just the money I wanted, was it? It was revenge. I want them to know I got back at them, and not a goddam thing they can do about it."

"You're just gonna disappear."

"It's happened."

"Less than it used to," Parker told him. "Right now I'm

sitting here listening to you instead of getting to some other part of the country because I don't have any safe ID."

"Well, you stirred them up," Lindahl said. "You robbed their bank."

"Robbing their track will stir them up, too."

"Let me tell you the idea," Lindahl said. "The way the track operates, the losers pay the winners, so the track never has to start off with cash. They take in enough from the first race to pay the winners, plus some more, and go from there. The track take is about twenty percent, that's the piece I'm after. At the end of the day, the cash and the credit card slips are all put in boxes and on carts, and the carts ride down to the basement in the freight elevator. They're wheeled down the corridor to what they call the safe room, because it's all concrete block, no windows, and only the one door that's metal and kept locked. Just past that is the door to the ramp that comes up to ground level at the end of the clubhouse. That door is kept locked, and the gate at the top of the ramp is kept locked. Monday through Friday, the armored car comes an hour after the track closes, backs down the ramp, loads on the day's take. Saturday and Sunday they don't come at all, and they don't show up until eight Monday morning, when they pick up the whole weekend's take."

"So your idea," Parker said, "is go in there Sunday night."

Lindahl shook his head. "Saturday night," he said. "Those boxes are heavy. Once the pallet is put down there on

Saturday, it isn't touched again till Monday morning. I go in there Saturday night with boxes look just like their boxes, because I know their boxes. I take the full ones, I leave the empty ones. Now I've got thirty-six hours before anybody knows anything. How far could I get in thirty-six hours, spending only cash, leaving no trail?"

Everybody leaves a trail, but there was no point explaining things to Lindahl, since it was all a fantasy, anyway. Parker might be able to make use of Lindahl's access if things were quieter around here and if he could collect a string of two or three sure guys, but there was no way for Lindahl himself to reach into that particular fire and not get burned.

It wasn't Parker's job to tell an amateur he was an amateur, to remind him of things like a driver's license, license plates, fingerprints, or the suspicions created by spending cash in a credit card economy. So he said, "You gonna take the parrot with you?"

Lindahl was surprised at the abrupt change of subject, and then surprised again when he saw it wasn't a change of subject, after all. "I never thought about that," he said, and laughed at himself again. "Be on the lookout for a man and a parrot." Turning to look at the parrot as though he'd never noticed it before, he said, "That's who I am these last few years, isn't it? Who else is gonna get a parrot that doesn't talk?"

"Not at all?"

"Not a word."

Lindahl studied the parrot an instant longer, while the bird cocked his head to study Lindahl right back, then gave that up to start rooting under its feathers with its beak, eyes wide and blank as the buttons on a first Communion coat.

Turning back to Parker, Lindahl said, "That's how little I'm interested in talk, the last few years. I better not take him, but that's no hardship. I'll do fine on my own. I won't start any conversations. Is that one of yours?"

Lindahl had nodded at the television set. Parker leaned forward to look to his right at the screen, and filling it was some old mug shot of Nick Dalesia, who had been one of his partners until just now. Nicholas Leonard Dalesia it said across the bottom of the screen.

So they had Nick. That changed everything.

"You want the sound on?"

"We know what they're saying," Parker said.

Lindahl nodded. "I guess we do."

A perp walk showed. Dalesia, wrists cuffed, head bowed, looking roughed up, moved in jerky quick steps from a state trooper car across a broad concrete sidewalk to the side entrance of a brick building in some county seat where this was the courthouse up front and the jail around on the side. New York State Police, so Nick, too, hadn't gotten very far. As many uniformed state troopers as could do it squeezed into the picture to hustle Nick along from the car to the building.

Parker leaned back, not looking at the set. Three of them had pulled the job and stowed the cash away rather than try to get it through the roadblocks. It was a given that if one of them got nabbed, that one would turn up the cash as a way to make his legal troubles a little easier. You might give up your partners, too, if you knew enough about them. Give the law anything you could if you were the first grabbed. Otherwise, don't get grabbed at all, because there was nothing left to trade.

So the money was gone. It had been a rich haul, but now it was gone, except for the four thousand in Parker's pocket, and he still had to work his way out of this minefield. He said, "You say the meet's going on now, at this track of yours?"

"Two more weeks," Lindahl said, "then shut down until late April."

"So there's three Saturdays left, today and two more."

"We couldn't do it tonight," Lindahl said, looking startled.

"We can go there tonight," Parker told him. "A dry run, see if it's possible."

Lindahl looked both eager and alarmed. "You mean, you'd work with me on this?"

"We'll look at it," Parker said.

four

Parker stood and crossed to the door, then raised the blind covering the window next to it. The boarded-up house standing between here and the road was a two-and-a-half-story wood-framed structure, probably one hundred years old, its original color long since time-bleached down to gray. Every door and window, except one small round window in the attic, was covered by large sheets of plywood, themselves also gray with age. Parker said, "Tell me about that place."

Lindahl got up to come over and stand beside him, saying, "A woman named Grothe lived there, forever. She was retired from somewhere in state government, lived there by herself, she was in her nineties when she finally died."

"Why's it boarded up?"

"Some cousins inherited the place, had nothing to do with this part of the world, gave it to a real estate agent to sell, years ago. But nobody's buying anything around here, so after a while the town took it over for taxes, boarded it up to keep the bums out."

"Ever been inside it?"

"Can't. It's sealed up. And who'd want to? Nothing in there but dust and dry rot."

"Who do you rent this place from?"

"The town. It's goddam cheap, and it oughta be. Who's this?"

A black Taurus had turned in from the road, was driving past the boarded-up house, headed this way. Lindahl gave Parker a quick look: "Are you here?"

When there's no place to hide, stand where you are. Parker said, "I'm Ed Smith, I used to work with you years ago at the track, I moved to Chicago, I'm back for a visit."

"Smith?"

"There are people named Smith," Parker said as a heavyset man in a maroon windbreaker got out of the car. "Who's he?"

"Oh, yeah," Lindahl said as the man shut the car door, glanced at Lindahl's Ford parked beside him, and started forward. "What the hell is his name? Fred, Fred something."

Fred saw them both in the window and waved. Under a red billed cap, his face was broad and thick, dominated by a ridge of bone horizontally above his eyes.

"Rod and Gun Club," Lindahl said, and opened the door. "Fred! Jesus, it's been years."

"You're still on the rolls," Fred said, and gave a quick nod and grin at Parker.

"Come in, come in," Lindahl said, stepping back from the doorway. "This is Ed Smith, he's visiting. You aren't after me for dues, are you?"

Fred gave that a dutiful laugh and stuck his hand out to Parker, saying, "Fred Thiemann. You a hunter, Ed?"

"Sometimes."

"I can offer you a beer," Lindahl said, sounding doubtful.

"No, no, no drinking," Fred said, "not at a time like this. You know about those bank robbers come over from Massachusetts."

Parker could sense the strain in Lindahl's neck muscles as he didn't turn to look at Parker, but instead said, "They caught one of them, didn't they?"

"Not that far from here. The state police figure the other two are holed up in this area someplace, so they sent out a request, American Legion and VFW posts, outfits like ours, just take a walk around any woods or empty spaces we've got, see do we turn up anything. It's the weekend, so we're getting a big turnout." He shrugged, grinning with both delight and embarrassment. "Like a bunch of kids, playing cops and robbers."

"Like a posse," Lindahl said.

"Exactly," Fred said. "Except, no horses. Anyway, a bunch of us are meeting at St. Stanislas, we'll look around the Hickory Hill area. Nobody expects to find anything, but we might help keep those guys on the run."

Parker said, "How'd they catch the first one?"

“He tried spending the bank’s money,” Fred said. “Turns out most of that was new cash, they had the serial numbers.”

The four thousand dollars in Parker’s pocket was new money. He said, “That guy was careless.”

“Let’s hope the other two are just as careless,” Fred said. “We didn’t have a phone number for you, Tom, so I said I’d come over on the way, see do you want to come along. You, too, Ed.”

Lindahl looked at Parker. “Would you want to do that?”

“Sure,” Parker said. “The safest place around is gonna be with the posse.”

five

"Tom," Parker said, "you'll have to loan me a rifle. I didn't bring one."

Lindahl gave him a startled look, but then said, "Sure. Come on in and pick one."

Fred Thiemann said, "Want me to wait for you boys?"

"No, you go on ahead," Lindahl told him. "It'll take me a couple minutes to get ready. I'll see you at St. Stanislas."

"Fine. Good to meet you, Ed."

"You, too."

Thiemann left, pulling the door shut behind himself, as Lindahl turned toward the bedroom. Parker followed, and when he stepped through the doorway, Lindahl was glaring at him, face suddenly blotched purple.

"You get out of here!" It was a hoarse whisper, almost a choked scream. "As soon as Fred drives off, you clear out!"

"No," Parker said.

"What?" Lindahl couldn't believe it. "You can't stay here, you're a fugitive!"

"We've got our agreement," Parker told him. "We'll stick to it."

"We will not! Not for another second."

Parker looked from the bedroom doorway out through the front window. "Fred just drove off," he said. "What are you going to do, holler? At that empty house up there? Are you going to try to take down one rifle and not two?"

"When you said – when you said, give me a rifle – Jesus, I came to my senses, right then and there. You could kill people I know."

"If I'm the only man there without a rifle," Parker said, "how does that look? What am I there for?"

Lindahl dropped backward to sit on the bed, hands limp between his knees. "I was out of my mind," he said, talking at the floor. "Brooding about that goddam track for so many years, then thinking about you, and by God if you don't show up, and I was just running a fantasy. A fantasy." Glaring at Parker, trying to look stern, he said, "I'm not giving any fantasy a rifle. You just take off. I got you this far, you're on your own. I won't say a word about you."

"Doesn't work," Parker told him. "You're accessory after the fact. You took me off that hill, you drove me home, you introduced me as somebody visiting with you. You show up at this saint place without me, what do you say to Fred? And what if I am caught, and Fred sees my picture on the television? What do you tell the cops?"

"I was crazy," Lindahl whispered, as though to himself. "I don't know what I was thinking."

"Revenge. I'm not going to shoot your friends, now that you've suddenly got all of them. I'll carry a rifle because that's what everybody's doing."

Lindahl looked at him. "What if we find the other guy? What if you're trying to help him get away?"

"I wouldn't try to help him get away," Parker said.

Lindahl frowned at him, trying to understand what he meant, and then his entire body slumped. "You mean, you'd kill him."

Parker would, to protect himself, but he didn't want Lindahl thinking about that. "I'll keep away from him," he said. "And he'll keep away from me. He's probably long gone from here, anyway."

Lindahl seemed unable to move forward. He continued to sit on the bed, staring at nothing at all, slowly shaking his head, as Parker went to study the four rifles in their locked racks on the wall.

The top two were nearly identical, Remington Model 1100, single barrel shotguns, the top one a 20-gauge, the other the slightly longer and heavier 16-gauge. The other two were both lever-action rifles, one a Marlin 336Y, firing a .30-30 Winchester cartridge, the other a Ruger 96, firing the .44 Magnum. All four weapons were old but well cared for, and might have been bought used.

Parker turned back to Lindahl, still slumped unmoving on the bed. "Lindahl," he said.

Lindahl looked up. There was very little emotion in

his eyes, so he was scheming down inside himself somewhere.

Parker said, "You and me, we'll go with this posse crowd. We'll take the two lever actions, no round in the chamber, that way neither of us can get off a snap shot. We'll stay with those people as long as they're out there, then we'll eat something and come back here."

"I don't want you here," Lindahl said, dull but stolid.

"Listen to me. We're talking a few hours out there. What you wanted – what you thought you wanted – was revenge. You'll have those hours to think about it. When we get back here, you tell me, either you still want to take down that track or you don't. If you do, we'll go look at it. If you don't, I'll leave in the morning."

"I don't want you here."

"You've got me. You brought me here, and you've got me. If it wasn't for your friend Fred, I could lock you in your utility room and not worry about you. But if we don't show up at this saint place, Fred's going to start wondering this and that. So we've got to do it. Let's go."

Lindahl shook his head in a slow dumbfounded way. "How did this happen?" he wanted to know.

"You made your choice when you saw me come up the hill," Parker told him. "Back then, you could have shot me, or held me there for the dogs, figuring there's got to be a reward. But you looked at me and said, 'This guy can help me.' Maybe I can. Or maybe you'll change your mind. We'll know when we get back. Do you have a spare coat? Something right for the woods?"

Lindahl blinked at him, confused. "A coat? I have a couple coats."

"And boots, if you've got them. These shoes aren't much use outdoors. Do you have extra boots?"

Lindahl didn't want to be dragged away into this other conversation. "I have boots, I have boots," he muttered, shaking his head. "But no. Take my car. Just drive away."

"Right into their arms," Parker said. "Look at me, Tom."

Reluctantly Lindahl looked up.

Parker said, "Do you want me to think you're trouble, Tom?"

Lindahl frowned, looking at him, then his eyes shifted away and he shook his head. "No."

"So you'll loan me a coat and a pair of boots. And you want the Ruger or the Marlin?"

six

The red and black wool coat was loose, but the lace-up boots fit well. Parker carried the Marlin, a thirty-four-inch-long single-shot rifle weighing six and a half pounds, with a five-shot tubular magazine. They put both rifles on the floor behind the front seat and drove away from Pooley, not the way they'd come in. They'd gone about six miles when they reached the first roadblock, two state police cars narrowing the road to one lane, cars and troopers sharply sketched in the late afternoon October sunlight against the dark surrounding woods.

As they slowed, Parker said, "You'll talk."

"I know."

The trooper who bent to Lindahl's open window was an older man, heavyset, taken off desk duty for this emergency and not happy about it. Lindahl told him his name and his membership in Hickory Rod and Gun, and that they were on their way to St. Stanislas to join the search.

The trooper stepped back to look in the rear side window at the rifles on the floor and said, "Whole county's filling up with untrained men with guns. Not how I'd do it, but nobody asked me. You got your membership card?"

"In the Rod and Gun Club? Sure." Reaching for his wallet, Lindahl sounded sheepish as he said, "It's a little out of date."

"Doesn't matter," the trooper said. "Doesn't have a photo, anyway." He nodded at the card Lindahl showed him, without taking it, and said, "Leave it on the dashboard so if you're stopped again they'll know who you are."

"Good idea." Lindahl put his membership card on top of the dashboard where it could be seen through the windshield.

The trooper, sour but resigned, stepped back and said, "Okay, go ahead."

"Thank you, sir."

They drove on, through hilly country, still mostly forested, many of the trees now changing to their fall colors, crimson and russet and gold. There were apple orchards, darkly red, and scruffy fields where dairy cows had once grazed, now mostly vacant, though here and there were groups of horses or sheep or even llamas. The houses were few and old and close to the ground.

They climbed awhile, the road switching back and forth through the partly tamed forest, then came to a town with a sign reading St. Stanislas and a steep main street. What they were headed for was not a church, but an old Grange Hall, its clapboard sides painted a medium brown too many years ago, with the metal signs of half a dozen fraternal organizations on stakes along the roadside out front.

A dozen cars were already in the parking lot beside the building, and Lindahl put the Ford in with them. They got their rifles, then walked over to where a group of men milled around the closed front door. They were mostly over fifty, hefty and soft, and they moved with checked-in excitement.

Lindahl knew all of these people, though it was clear he hadn't seen any of them for some time. They were pleased to see him, if not excited, and pleased to meet Parker as well, introduced as an old friend of Lindahl's here on a visit.

Parker shook hands with the smiling men who were hunting him, and then a state police car arrived and two uniformed men got out, the younger one an ordinary trooper, the older one with extra braid and insignia on his uniform and hat.

This is the one who went up on the steps leading to the Grange Hall and turned around to say, "I want to thank you gentlemen for coming out today. We have two very dangerous men somewhere in our part of the world, and it's an act of good citizenship to help find them and put them under control. You've all heard on the television the crime they committed. They didn't kill anybody, but they caused a great deal of property damage and put three armored-car employees in the hospital. The weapons they used are banned in the United States. We don't know if they're still carrying those weapons, or if they might have others as well. We do know they were armed and are extremely dangerous. We ask that no one go off by himself, but always have at least one other person from your group in sight. If you come across one or both of these fugitives, do not try to apprehend them yourselves. These are professional criminals, desperate men facing long prison sentences, and they have no reason not to shoot you down if you get in their way. If you believe you've found them, get that information to us or to some other authority at the earliest possible moment. Try to keep them in sight, and do not under any circumstances exchange gunfire with them. Trooper Oskott has artist's drawings of the two men that we'll pass among you, and then your club president, Ben Weiser, will describe to you the area we'd like you to patrol. Ben?"

Ben Weiser was a man in his sixties, as overweight as most of the rest of them, with absolutely no hair on the top of his head but very long gray hair down the sides and back, covering his ears and his collar, so that he looked like a retired cavalry scout. As Trooper Oskott moved among the group, handing out sheets of copy paper, Weiser said, "It's nice to see just about everybody here, and even an extra volunteer, Ed Smith over there, brought to us by Tom Lindahl, so I guess that makes up for all the times Tom didn't show up. Glad you're here, Tom. Welcome to Hickory Rod and Gun Club, Ed."

Parker took the two sheets the trooper handed him and looked at them while Weiser went on being folksy and another man went into the Grange Hall and came back out with an easel that he set up on the top step. The drawing of himself he'd seen before, on the television set in the diner before the law had arrived, attracted by his rental car. Nobody in the diner had looked from the screen to this customer among them and said, "There he is!" and nobody here in front of the Grange Hall turned to say, "Ed? Isn't this you?"

The other drawing, he knew, was supposed to be McWhitney, his partner back then, and if you knew McWhitney and had been told this was supposed to be him, you could see the similarities, but McWhitney himself could walk past this group right now and not one of them would give a second look.

Artist's drawings didn't bother Parker. What bothered him was the four thousand dollars in traceable cash in his pocket and the lack of a usable ID. Until he replaced both of those, the best place for him was right here with the search party.

"Tough-looking guys," somebody said. "I'm not sure I want to find them."

That got a laugh, and then somebody else said, "Oh, I think Cory and me could take 'em, couldn't we, Cory?"

"I'll hold your coat," the one next to him said, and while that got its own laugh, Parker looked at the two of them, Cory and the one whose coat he'd hold.

They were a little younger than most in the group, a little rougher-looking, both dressed in jeans and boots and dark heavy work shirts. They might have been brothers, with the same thick dark blond hair hanging straggly around their ears, the same easy slope of the shoulders. The one who thought he and Cory could take the fugitives had a black patch over his left eye, which inevitably gave him a piratical look, as though he were the tougher brother. With that eye, now, he peered around at the group, slightly challenging, watching out for somebody else he could take. His good eye brushed past Parker, and Parker looked away, not needing to be noticed too much.

Meanwhile, up in front of them, Ben Weiser said, "Here's a government survey map," which somebody had put on the easel, but then had to hold there because otherwise the breeze would blow it off. Weiser then went on to describe what area they were expected to search in, saying things like, "You know the old Heisler place," which they all did.

Parker paid little attention to the details, because this wasn't a part of the country he knew, but it was interesting to see the approach they had taken. They were guessing that the men they wanted would have left the main roads, and possibly the secondary roads as well, though why they should think bank robbers were woodsmen wasn't clear. But the approach was to cover back roads and dirt roads and dead-end roads that weren't used any more, and particularly to cover abandoned buildings, old farmhouses and barns, and even a railroad station up where a town no longer existed because its iron mine had given out more than a century ago.

Which was where Parker would be searching, along with Tom Lindahl and Fred Thiemann. The decision had been made that the search parties should consist of groups of three, and Weiser explained the reason. If they did come across one or both of the fugitives, one of their group could go off to raise the alarm without leaving one man alone to keep the quarry in sight.

The men, who had arrived here separately or in pairs, now sorted themselves into threes and headed for the cars. Lindahl's SUV was roomier than Thiemann's Taurus, so they'd use that, with Lindahl driving, Parker beside him as before, and Thiemann in back with the rifles.

They joined the exodus from the Grange Hall parking lot, followed a couple of other cars for the first mile or so, and Lindahl explained, "This place we're going to, called Wolf Peak, was a mining town way back when."

"Before the Civil War," Thiemann put in from the backseat. "The whole Northeast was iron mines, but the Civil War used it all up."

"Wolf Peak went on till the end of the century," Lindahl said, "with the tailings, and some lumbering, but the younger generations kept moving away, and when the railroad stopped going up there, around 1900, that was the end."

Thiemann said, "The houses were all wood, so they burned or rotted, but the railroad station was good local stone. The roof's gone, but the walls are solid. I hunkered down in there myself once, out hunting and here comes a thunderstorm."

"There might be a couple other hidey-holes up around there," Lindahl said, "but mostly it's the railroad station."

Spreading himself comfortably across the backseat, Thiemann said, "What I'm guessing about these robbers, I'm guessing they're city people, and they aren't gonna know what it means to try to hide out in a place like this."

Parker said, "How's that?"

"People like Tom and me," Thiemann said, "we been here generations, it's like we got our grandparents' memories mixed in with our own. We know this chunk of the planet Earth. No city person's gonna know a city like we know these hills. A stranger tries to move through here, tries to hide out in here, somebody's gonna see him and say, 'That fella doesn't belong.' You can't hide around here."

"I see what you mean," Parker said.

Leaning forward a little, Thiemann said, "Where you living these days, Ed?"

"Chicago," Parker told him. "I don't know it very well."

Thiemann grinned. "You know what I mean, then," he said, and sat back.

Their road trended mainly uphill, and a few miles later crossed a larger road, where a police presence had been set up. The trooper this time, a younger one than the first, walked over, saw Lindahl's membership card on the dash, and waved them through. Grinning, he called, "Happy hunting!"

A few miles later Lindahl made a left onto a road, a two-lane blacktop in crumbling condition, that angled steeply up. "There's a couple houses just up ahead," he said, "that they keep the blacktop for. After that, it's dirt."

"Shake the teeth right out of your head," Thiemann commented.

He was close to right. After the second small occupied house, the woods settled in closer on both sides, the hill grew even steeper, and the surface they drove over was more corrugation than road. Lindahl drove slowly, trying to steer around the deepest holes.

Parker said, "Was the railroad line near the road? I don't see any sign of it."

"They pulled up the tracks for scrap during World War Two," Lindahl told him. "It's only a couple more miles now."

First there were stubs of wall, stone or brick, in among the tree trunks on both sides of the road, then a couple of collapsed wooden buildings, crumpled down to a third of their original height, and then, ahead on the right, the railroad station, squat and long, roofless, with narrow tall window sockets and remnants of a concrete skirt around its base. Maple and cherry trees had grown up inside the station, some taller than the roofline. The woods on this slope were so thick that only narrow angles of sunlight reached the ground, like spotlights that had lost the performer they were supposed to follow.

Whatever level parking area had once existed around the station was long overgrown. Lindahl simply stopped on the rutted road in front of the building, and all three got out. Thiemann carried his rifle, a bolt-action Winchester 70 in .30-06, while Lindahl opened the left rear door and took out both of the other rifles. Parker walked around the front of the Ford, held his hand out, and after a second, Lindahl, with a strong and mistrustful frown, gave him the Marlin.

Vines covered part of the building, including hanging down over the doorless front entrance. "You want to be careful with that," Thiemann said, pointing toward the doorway. "That's poison ivy."

"There's probably wider doors around back," Lindahl said, "for freight."

They walked around the building, and there was really nothing at all any more to say what it had originally been, no platforms, no railbed, no rotting luggage carts. The place might have started, long before, as a temple in the jungle.

One of the doorways on this side was broad, and clear of vines. They stepped through, and Thiemann pointed to the left, saying, "That's where I hunkered down that time, waiting for the storm to go away." Then he peered more closely at that corner and said, "What's that?"

They moved into the building, toward the left corner, and a little stack of old cloth had been piled there, ragged old blankets and towels. It looked like a mouse nest, but it had been put together by a man.

"You're not the only one got out of the storm here," Lindahl said. Looking up, he said, "It's the best protected spot, I guess, with those tree branches."

Bracing himself with his rifle butt against the root and dirt floor, Thiemann squatted down and felt the pile of cloth with his left palm. Solemn, wide eyed, he looked up and mouthed, just barely loud enough to be heard, "Warm."

Lindahl stared at Parker. His hands were clenched tight on his rifle, the way they'd been the first time Parker had seen him, on the hill ahead of the dogs.

Parker said, "Heard the car coming."

Thiemann stood. "He's nearby, then." He was excited, almost giddy, but trying hard to hide it, to seem mature and professional.

Lindahl, speaking mostly to Parker, said, "Do you guess he's armed?"

"Not if he was trying to get through roadblocks."

"If he's holed up in here," Thiemann said, "he isn't getting through any roadblocks."

Parker knew this wouldn't be McWhitney they'd found, but had no reason to say so. "Could be somebody else," he said.

Thiemann scoffed at that. "Way the hell up in here?"

"Could be you, once."

Thiemann shook his head, getting irritated at having his fantasy poked at. Pointing at the pile of cloth, he said, "I didn't make myself a bunk, and" – finger pointing skyward – "there's no thunderstorm. So let's take a look at what we got up here."

They left the station, Thiemann going first at a half-crouch, rifle ready in both hands in front of himself. Outside, he stopped and looked across the space where the tracks would have been, and into the woods. He had become very still, all eyes and ears, studying that wild land over there, sloped steeply down to the right, clogged with low shrubs in among the narrow trunks of the second-growth forest.

Parker and Lindahl waited, a pace behind Thiemann, and after a long minute Thiemann took a backward step toward them, without looking away from the woods. "You see where I'm looking."

Ahead, and just to the right. Parker and Lindahl looked there, too. Parker didn't know if Lindahl saw anything, but he didn't; just more shrubs and more trees.

"Little branches broken on that multiflora there," Thiemann murmured. "That stuff's miserable to get through. See how he forced his way?"

"You know, I do," Lindahl said. "Very good, Fred."

"Not that different from hunting a deer." Thiemann nodded at the woods. "You two flank me left and right, I'll go through where he went through."

They set off slowly, Lindahl giving Parker one quick worried look behind Thiemann' s back, but then concentrating on the terrain ahead.

The land was broken, tilted, full of rocks; very slow going. There was no way to be quiet about it, their feet crunching on old leaves and fallen branches, their bodies shoving branches out of the way. They moved about ten yards forward, and when Parker looked back, the lower part of the station building was already obscured by the undergrowth, only the uneven roofline still visible. It wouldn't take long to get lost in here.

"Freeze!"

That was Thiemann, a dim uncertain shape through the woods to Parker's left.

A sudden loud rustle and clatter ahead of them was someone running, running desperately through the unforgiving forest.

"Fred, hold it!" That was Lindahl, invisible beyond Thiemann, sounding panicky.

"Halt, goddammit!" Thiemann again.

The sound of the shot was a dead flat crack in the open air, like two blocks of wood slapped together, without echo.

"Fred, don't!"

Too late; there was one hoarse scream, and then a great turbulence on the forest floor. Parker moved forward toward that thrashing. To his left, Thiemann moved more cautiously, bent low.

Whatever had been hit was now lunging around out there, agitating the shrubbery, making a racket. Parker got to him in time to see the blood still bubble from the hole in the man's back, the color of wine, the thickness of motor oil. The man, facedown on the leaves and branches, jerked his arms and legs as though swimming through the woods.

And then he stopped. The blood from the hole in his back bubbled less, and pulsed to an end as Thiemann arrived, panting as though he'd run a mile. He stared at the man on the ground as intently as if he'd just given him birth. His voice hoarse, he said, "Which one is he?"

"Neither," Parker said.

Lindahl came to join them, from farther to the left. "How is he?"

"Dead," Parker said.

Thiemann was trying to get the artist's drawings out of his pocket without letting go of his rifle. "Damn," he said. "Damn! Tom, hold this a sec."

Lindahl took Thiemann's rifle, and Thiemann got out the two papers, unfolded them, and went down on one knee beside the dead man. He was clearly reluctant to touch the body, but had to turn the head in order to see the face.

"He's not one of them," Parker said.

Thiemann wasn't ready for that, not yet. This man on the ground in front of them was small, scrawny, old, with thin gray filthy hair and a thick gray untended beard. He wore tattered gray work pants and a moth-eaten old blue sweater, stained everywhere. Lace up black shoes too big for him were on his feet, without socks, the ankles dirty and scabbed from old cuts.

The face, when Thiemann used both hands to turn the dead man's head, was bone thin, deeply lined, with scabs around the mouth and under the eyes. The eyes stared in horror at something a long way off.

Thiemann squirmed backward, rubbing his fingers on grass and leaves. "He's some old bum," he said. His voice sounded the way the dead man's staring eyes looked.

Lindahl said, "Fred? You didn't get a good look at him?"

"He was . . . running. What the hell was he running for?"

Parker said, "Men with guns chased him."

"Shit." Thiemann was trying to find some rope to grasp, something, some way to get his balance back. "Doesn't he know? The whole countryside knows. Everybody's out looking for the bank robbers. Nobody wants him, what the hell's he running for?" He stood leaning, looking at nothing, arms at his sides.

Lindahl said gently, "Fred, that guy wasn't up on the news. He's up in here, he's some old wino, he goes down sometimes and cadges or steals, but he doesn't keep up with current events, Fred."

Thiemann said, "I'm feeling, I can't, I gotta . . ."

Parker and Lindahl grabbed him, one on each side, and eased him down until he was seated on the ground, the dead man just to his left. Not looking in that direction, he pushed himself around in a quarter circle until he was faced away from the body. "Do you think," he said, much more humbly than before, "do you think we should bring – it – him, bring him out? Or should we just tell the troopers where he is?"

"No," Parker said.

Thiemann looked up. "What?"

"We don't tell the troopers," Parker said. "We don't tell anybody."

Lindahl was holding his own rifle in his right hand, Thiemann's in his left. Looking warily toward Parker, moving as though he wished that left hand were free, he said, "What do you mean, Ed?"

"They told us," Parker said, "don't exchange gunfire. Even if this was one of them, we weren't supposed to shoot. He isn't one of them, he isn't armed, he was shot in the back." Parker looked at Thiemann. "If you go to the troopers with this, you'll do time."

"But—" Thiemann stared left and right, looking for exits. "That isn't right. We're like deputies."

"Search," Parker said. "Observe. Don't engage. If you go to the law, Fred, it's bad for you, and it's bad for us."

That snagged Thiemann's attention. "Bad for you? Jesus, how is this bad for you?"

Parker could not have the law interested in this trio of hunters. He wouldn't survive five minutes of being looked at by the law in a serious way. But what Thiemann needed was a different reason. "You shot an unarmed man in the back," he said, to twist that knife a little. "A man who isn't one of the ones we're looking for. Tom and I were right here with you, and we didn't stop you. That means we're part of it." Looking at Lindahl, Parker said, without moving his rifle, "You know what I'm saying, Tom. It's just as important for us. This thing didn't happen."

Lindahl, face paler than before, understood both what Parker was telling him and what Parker was telling Thiemann. He said, "My God, Ed, you mean, just leave him here? You can't do that to a human being."

"Tom," Parker said, "what that guy was doing to himself was just as bad, only slower. He didn't have much of a life, and there wasn't a lot of it left. What difference does it make if he dies back there in that ruin from exposure or starvation or DTs or liver poisoning, or if he dies out here from Fred's bullet? He's dead, and the animals around here'll take care of the body."

"Jesus," Fred said, and put his shaking left hand up to cover his eyes.

"I can't even think that way," Lindahl said.

"I'm thinking for you," Parker told him. "This is a bind we're in, and the only way out of it is that it didn't happen."

Lindahl looked helplessly at the dead man, at the huddled shape of Thiemann, at Parker. "Should we at least . . . bury him?"

Parker scuffed his toe on the stony ground. "In this? How? Even if we had three shovels, and we don't, it would take hours to make a hole in this ground. And what for? Fred, what animals you got up around here, besides deer?"

Thiemann seemed surprised to be spoken to. Slowly he took his hand away from his eyes and squinted upward, toward Parker, but not quite meeting his eye. "Animals?"

"Predators. Scavengers."

Thiemann sighed, long and shuddering, but when he spoke, his voice was calm. "Well," he said, "we got coyote, not a whole lot, but some."

"Bobcat," Lindahl said.

"That's right," Thiemann agreed, and gestured skyward. "And a whole lot of turkey buzzards."

"They'll get here," Lindahl said, "right after we leave."

Thiemann shook his head. "Well, no," he said, "not that fast. A few hours later, it's gotta get—" He stopped, squeezed his eyes shut, shook his head. "God damn!"

"You thought it was the right guy," Parker told him. Now that Thiemann wouldn't be any more trouble, it was best that he not get excited. "It could have happened to any of us."

"That's right, Fred," Lindahl said.

Thiemann spread his hands. "I was just so— I thought, Wow, I've got him! Me! I've got him!" He shook his head again, disgusted with himself. "When I said we were acting like kids, I didn't really mean it, I thought it was a joke. It wasn't a joke." Looking now toward Lindahl, he said, asking forgiveness, "I never killed a man before. A human being. I never killed anybody. Deer, you've got venison, you've got . . ."

"A reason," Lindahl suggested.

"I'm not sure I can even do that any more." Thiemann looked around, but not toward the body. "Would you guys help me up?"

They did, and he said, "I can't do this any more, I gotta go home, I gotta, I don't know, get by myself somewhere. I can't do this today."

Parker said, "You got a wife at home, Fred?"

"Sure," Thiemann said, "and one daughter still in college."

"Can you tell your wife things? Can you trust her?"

That drew Thiemann's startled attention. "Sure I can trust her. But tell her about" – with a hand gesture behind himself, toward the corpse – "about that?"

"You've got to tell somebody," Parker said. "You can't put it where you can't ever talk about it, because it'll eat you up. You won't last. And you can't talk about it with anybody else, not even Tom here. Tell your wife, talk it out with her."

"He's right, Fred," Lindahl said. "Jane will help you."

Thiemann made an awkward shrug, uncomfortable with himself. "Get me back to my car, will you?"

They started back through the thick shrubbery toward the ruined railroad station. Thiemann hadn't asked for his rifle back, seemed not to want to know it was his, so Lindahl carried them both under his right arm, leaving his left arm free to push through the branches along the way.

Parker lagged behind the other two a pace, watched their backs, and decided what to do about them. The continued roadblocks in this part of the world, his lack of usable ID, even his lack of usable cash, meant he had to stick with Lindahl if possible, at least for now.

But how reliable was Thiemann? If he did talk with his wife, and if she was sensible, if she understood what was best to keep him out of trouble, it should be all right. But if Thiemann started to talk to anybody else, anybody at all, it would unravel in a minute. And Parker wouldn't know there was a problem until Lindahl's house was surrounded.

The other choice was to shoot them both, take Lindahl's Ford, get away from here. Until he left this county, Lindahl's membership card in Hickory Rod and Gun Club, displayed on the dashboard, would get him through the police blocks, particularly if he left the rifle prominently on the backseat. Not the Marlin, Lindahl's Ruger, the only weapon here that would not have been fired.

But the trouble wasn't just this county. The trouble extended for a hundred miles in every direction. To have a place to hole up was the most valuable asset he could hope for right now. If either Lindahl or Thiemann looked enough like him to make it possible to use their identification, it would be a different thing.

Lindahl suddenly turned his head, frowning at Parker

with a question in his eyes, but Parker was simply pushing through the brush like the other two, the Marlin held loose in the crook of his right arm, hand nowhere near the lever or the trigger. Parker nodded at him, expressionless, and Lindahl faced the station, just ahead of them now, and pushed on.

seven

They sat in the Ford the same as before, Lindahl driving, Parker beside him, Thiemann in the back with the three guns. The first few minutes, driving down the washboard road, no one spoke, but then Thiemann, as though he'd been brooding on this a long time, said, "I'm really in your hands now, aren't I? You guys."

Lindahl shot a quick glance at the rearview mirror but then had to watch the road. "In our hands? What do you mean, in our hands?"

"Well, you know this . . . thing about me. You know I killed a man."

Parker half turned so he could look at Thiemann, and rested his forearm atop the seat back. "We all have to trust each other, Fred. Tom and me, we're not reporting it, so that puts us in the same boat as you."

"Not exactly," Thiemann said, sounding bitter. "Not quite, Ed Smith. Not exactly."

With another quick look at the mirror, Lindahl said, "What's the matter, Fred? You know me. We've known each other a long time."

"Not for a long time, Tom," Thiemann told him. "Not for years. You don't come to meetings, you don't go anywhere. I haven't seen your face in three years. You're like a hermit."

"I'm not that bad," Lindahl said, but as though admitting that yes, maybe he was that bad.

"Everybody knows," Thiemann told him, "you turned sour when you lost your job."

Lindahl didn't like that. "Oh, do they? Everybody knows? Everybody talks about it a lot, do they, Fred?"

"Nobody has to talk about it," Thiemann said. "Everybody already knows. You lost that job, you turned sour, your wife walked out, you don't act like you're anybody's friend. I don't know you any more. I don't know you much more than I know this fella here, except I know he talks smooth and he talks fast."

"Fred," Parker said, "you just tell your wife, Jane, what happened today and see if she wants you to turn yourself in. If she does, it doesn't matter what I say."

"Oh, I know what she'll say," Thiemann said, as though the knowledge made him angry. "Keep out of trouble, don't make things worse, you can't bring that man back, it's over and done with."

"Absolutely right," Lindahl said.

Leaning forward, his face closer to Parker so he could

talk to Lindahl's profile, Thiemann said, "The one thing she won't tell me is forget it. I'm never gonna forget it."

Lindahl said, "None of us are, Fred. That was a bad moment for all of us."

Parker could see that Thiemann thought he was supposed to be punished now, but he was smart enough to understand he couldn't punish himself without punishing other people, too. First his wife, and the daughter still in college. But Tom Lindahl after that.

So what Thiemann was doing back there now was trying to separate himself from the other people who'd get hurt. Tom Lindahl was a stranger to him, a hermit who had turned sour. His wife wouldn't give him understanding, she'd just give him boilerplate stock responses. He couldn't think about these unworthy people, he could only think about himself.

The daughter would be harder to dismiss. That might hold him in place. In any case, the dangerous time was between now and when Thiemann reached his home. If his wife was there.

Parker said, "Fred, is your wife home now?"

"Yeah," Thiemann said without much interest. "She works at a hospital, but not on Saturdays."

"That's good," Parker said.

They drove in silence again until they were back down on the county road and along it to the intersection with the roadblock, where the smiling trooper recognized them and waved them through. Lindahl and Parker waved back, but Thiemann sat crouched into himself, staring at the back of the seat in front of him. Then, just after that, Thiemann roused himself and said, not to either of them in particular, "I don't know if I can drive."

Parker looked at him, and Thiemann's face was very pale now. He'd been in shock since it had happened, but the shock was just beginning to bite in, taking blood from the parts of him where it was needed, like his brain.

Lindahl said, "You want me to drive you home, Fred?"

"But then there's the car," Thiemann said, "way the hell in St. Stanislas."

Parker said, "I could drive you in your car, Fred, and Tom could follow and pick me up at your place."

Lindahl tossed a sharp look at Parker. "You mean, I follow right behind you."

Parker said, "That's the only way I'm gonna get back to your house, Tom. Fred, you want me to do that?"

Thiemann frowned at Parker, then at the back of Lindahl's head, then at Parker again. "I think so," he said. "I think I got to do that. Thanks."

eight

Several cars were in the Grange Hall parking lot, left by people doubling into another team member's car, as Thiemann had done. It looked as though no one else had come back yet. Among the vehicles parked here was a state police car. Seeing it, Parker said to Lindahl, "You talk to the trooper. I'll go with Fred to his car. Fred took sick after we checked out the railroad station. Nobody there."

"Okay."

The trooper was getting out of his car. It was the older one with the braid, who'd addressed the group before. Lindahl steered around to park next to Thiemann's Taurus, then they all got out onto the blacktop.

As Lindahl went off to talk with the trooper, Thiemann fumbled in his pocket for his keys, finally got them out, then couldn't get his fingers to work well enough to push the button that would unlock the doors. "Damn. I can't—"

"Give it to me."

Thiemann looked at Parker and didn't want to hand over his keys, but then he did. Parker buzzed the doors open and looked past the SUV hood to where Lindahl and the trooper were talking. Lindahl seemed to be doing the job right, with no problem from the trooper.

Thiemann opened the driver's door, then stood looking confused. "I should be on the other side," he said.

"I'll get your rifle," Parker said.

"No!"

It was a sharp response, loud enough to make both Lindahl and the trooper look this way. Calm, quiet, Parker said, "You want to leave it with Tom?"

Thiemann blinked, and nodded. "For now," he said. "Yeah, just for now. I'll pick it up . . . sometime."

"I'll tell him. You get in on the other side, I'll be right back."

"Yes, okay."

Carrying Thiemann's car keys, Parker walked over to Lindahl and the trooper, who were both still looking this way. "Afternoon," he said to the trooper.

"Afternoon. Everything all right there?"

"No, Fred's all loused up."

Lindahl said, "You ask me, he's got Lyme disease."

"Well, we've got a lot of that around here," the trooper said.

"Headache," Parker said, "and a lot of confusion. I'm gonna drive him home."

"Good idea."

"Tom, he says you should hold on to his rifle, he'll pick it up later." Parker shrugged, and offered the trooper a faint grin. "That was the 'no' he shouted," he said. "I think he's afraid he might accidentally shoot himself."

"Stumble with a rifle in your hands," the trooper said. "It's happened."

"Tom, you ready to follow me?"

"I think so. Okay, Captain?"

"Fine," the trooper said. "Thank you for your help."

"Anytime," Lindahl told him.

They started away, and the trooper called, "Tell your friend to get tested. You don't fool with Lyme disease."

"I'll tell him," Lindahl promised.

They walked on, and Parker said quietly, "I guess that's some sort of local disease around here."

"You get it from a tick in the woods," Lindahl told him. "It's a very mean disease. But you know, I bet Fred would rather have that right now than what he's got."

nine

Parker got behind the wheel of the Taurus, adjusted the seat for his longer legs, started the engine, and then looked at Thiemann, who sat slumped beside him, staring at nothing, deep in his own thoughts. Parker waited, then said, "Which way?"

"What? Oh. Christ, I don't know what's the matter with me."

"You got shook up," Parker told him. "It's natural. Which way?"

"Uh, left out of the parking lot."

Parker drove that way, seeing Lindahl's SUV steady in his rearview mirror. "If I'm gonna make a turn," he said, "tell me before I get to it."

"Yeah, I'm okay now. I'll be okay."

"Good."

They drove two miles, and Parker became aware that Thiemann's attention had gradually shifted from his own interior landscape to Parker's profile. Thiemann frowned at him, quizzical, seeming to try to understand something. Parker said nothing, and then Thiemann faced front and said, "There's a stop sign coming up. You'll turn right."

"Good."

They made the turn, and ahead was another roadblock. Parker lowered his window, eased over to the shoulder, and waved Lindahl to overtake him. When Lindahl did, his own passenger window open, Parker called to him, "We're with you, you've got our guns."

Lindahl nodded and drove ahead, Parker now following him. He said, "Tom know the way to your house?"

"Sure."

"Good. He can lead the way, you don't have to worry about telling me."

"Probably good."

Ahead, Lindahl slowed for the barricade. The cop there, local, not state, saw Lindahl's membership card on the dash and waved him through, but Lindahl stopped, long enough to give the message. The cop looked toward the rifles on the floor in back, then nodded, waved Lindahl through again, and did the same to Parker; not grinning like the other one, but not stopping him, either.

They drove on awhile in silence, trailing Lindahl now, and then Thiemann said, "You didn't like that roadblock."

"It's easier if they'll wave you through it. And we wanted Tom out front to lead me."

"Yeah, but you didn't like the roadblock."

"I don't like any roadblock," Parker said. "They make me nervous. People get tensed up, sometimes accidents happen."

"Nothing makes you nervous," Thiemann said.

Parker looked at him, then back at Lindahl up ahead.

"What's that supposed to mean?"

"I got the wind knocked out of me, up there, when I shot that guy."

"Sure you did."

"Tom felt it, too. But you didn't."

"Maybe I just don't show things that much."

"Maybe. But you were pretty cool. You knew what we should do and why we should do it. Tom and me, we wouldn't have thought to leave that poor guy up there for the scavengers to eat. The first thing you said to me, what scavenger animals do we have around here?"

"Because you were in trouble, Fred," Parker told him. "You know you were. And Tom knows it, too."

"The second you saw that roadblock," Thiemann said, "you were opening the window, getting off the road. You knew exactly what to say to Tom."

"It was easier to get waved through on Tom's ticket than have to stop and go through all that."

"Just show ID," Thiemann said.

"It was easier not to."

Thiemann looked out the windshield, not saying

anything more, but thinking it over. He was suspicious of something, but he didn't know what. He had sensed the otherness in Parker, but he didn't know what it meant.

An older Cadillac convertible, bright red, top down, big as a speedboat, came the other way, suddenly honking madly. The three guys in it, middle-aged, in their bright orange or red hunting caps, waved hands with beer cans in them at Lindahl, who honked and waved back but didn't stop. Neither did the Cadillac, which went on by, the three guys all grinning and shouting things, now at Parker and Thiemann. They were very happy. Parker nodded but didn't honk.

"That's part of our group," Thiemann said.

"I know."

"They shouldn't be drinking. That's the worst thing you can do." Then Thiemann turned away with a grimace. "Almost the worst thing."

Ahead, Lindahl signaled for a left, and Parker did, too. "How much farther?"

"A couple miles." Thiemann turned toward him again. "You don't think much of us, do you?"

"How do you mean?"

"Not just those guys with the beer," Thiemann said. "All of us, running around, being man hunters. You could see in those troopers' eyes, they thought we were all just a joke. Useless, and a joke. And I could see it in your eyes, too. You think the same thing."

Parker followed Lindahl around the turn. Thiemann's sense of Parker's otherness, which had led him toward suspicion, had now led him to embarrassment instead; Parker wasn't an alien from outside them, unknown and untrusted, he was a judge from above them, finding them wanting. Good; that moved Thiemann away from a direction that might have caused trouble.

"Isn't that right, Ed? You think the same thing?"

"Not a joke," Parker said. "You just don't have the training. I suppose, if you'd been trained, up there in the woods, you wouldn't have moved quite so fast."

"Not quite so fast." Thiemann barked a laugh with no amusement in it. "You'd think, with the training, the trained guy'd be faster."

"The trained guy knows when to be fast," Parker said.

"You trained, Ed?"

"Some."

"I thought so. It's here."

This area was more suburban than country, with curving roads flanked by neat small houses on large green lots. Lindahl, signaling for a right, didn't turn but came to a stop just beyond a driveway. At the other end of the driveway was a tan stucco ranch with attached two-car garage.

Parker, turning in at the driveway, said, "Which garage?"

"Doesn't matter, they're both full of junk."

Parker stopped, switched off the engine, and opened his

door. But Thiemann went on just sitting there. Parker said, "The sooner you talk to her, the better."

"What the hell am I gonna say?"

"Honey, I made a mistake today."

Thiemann's expression was haggard. "That's a hell of a way to put it."

"It's what happened."

"A mistake."

"Let's get out of the car."

They got out of the Taurus and looked at each other across its top. "I keep thinking," Thiemann said, "it's a good thing for me you didn't get impatient. I don't know why I keep thinking that."

"I got nothing but patience," Parker told him. "I'm on vacation. Go talk to your wife."

"I will. Maybe I'll see you around, before you leave."

"Maybe," Parker said.

ten

Parker got into the Ford, and Lindahl immediately shifted into drive. Then, looking at the empty suburban street as it curved away in front of them, he said, "How is he?"

"You know him better than I do."

"Not in something like this." Lindahl gave Parker a quick uneasy look, as though not sure how to explain himself, then faced the road. "This isn't something that just happened," he said. "He shot a man. I can't even imagine that."

"You tried to stop him."

"He was just too—" Lindahl paused while he turned out of the suburb onto a country road. "Fred likes to be in charge," he said. "He likes to think he's the guy can take care of it, whatever it is."

"Can he take care of what he's got now?"

Another quick glance. "What do you mean?"

"He's in shock," Parker said. "So right now he doesn't know what he's thinking. Also, down inside, he has the idea he ought to be punished. That could lead him to the law, which would be bad for everybody."

"Especially you."

"No, especially Fred. He may like to pretend he's in charge, but he's in foreign territory now. His grandfather's memories aren't gonna help him."

Lindahl snorted. "I bet he's sorry he said that."

"Maybe, later."

"I'll tell you something could help him," Lindahl said, "that he wouldn't ever talk about. His oldest son is in jail."

"How did that happen?"

"He was in the army, they sent him to the Middle East, teach those people all about democracy. He met a couple young local guys taught him a few things of their own. These are fellas walk into your house, walk out with stuff they didn't have before."

"Uh-huh."

"Not like you. Small-time. Impressed George, though. He came back, he told everybody about them. They even had a special slang for them. Hawasim, it means looter." Lindahl shrugged. "I guess it's not as easy to be a looter in a war zone."

"Probably not."

"Young George thought he was hawasim himself, now he's doing three to five in Attica, the last thing Fred wants is to be in the next cell."

"Good."

They drove on, silent a while. Parker thought the shock of a son in prison must have been almost as strong for Thiemann as the second shock that had hit him today. Would the double hit make him likelier to withdraw into himself, stay quiet, not make trouble? Or would it make him spin out of control?

"I want to do it," Lindahl said.

There had been close to ten minutes of silence in the car, and now Lindahl spoke abruptly, as though not wanting to forget what he had to say. Or as though not wanting the chance to change his mind. The words had been forceful but flat, Lindahl's expression intense.

Parker said, "The track?"

"I hadn't seen any of those people for years," Lindahl said. "What'd Fred say? Three years? He's right, I don't know them any more, and they don't know me. They don't give a shit about me."

"They haven't seen you."

"They have an opinion about me," Lindahl said, "and that's all they need. You heard what Fred said. I lost my job, lost my wife, turned sour, end of story."

"You didn't give them any other story."

"Because it's true." Lindahl nodded at the road in front of them, agreeing with himself. "As long as I stay around here," he said, "I'm just what they think I am. A hermit, Fred said. Didn't destroy my life just the once, destroy it all over again every day." Another emphatic nod, this time with an emphatic glare in Parker's direction. "As long as I'm here," he said, "that's who I am, there's no hope I'll ever get out of this. I have to go down and take that money from the track because otherwise I'm dead here, I'm just walking around dead, all by myself." He laughed, a bitter sound. "With a parrot that doesn't talk."

"We'll drive down there," Parker said. "After dark."

Lindahl took a long shuddering inhale and slowly let it out. "I'm a new guy," he said. "I don't look it yet, but that's what I am."

eleven

With the sound off, the television set seemed to be saying that nothing much had happened. Parker gave Lindahl back his outer coat and boots, and then Lindahl went off to find some take-out food. "You don't want any of that rabbit I got," he said. "And neither do I, any more."

"Fine," Parker said.

Lindahl shrugged into his coat. "There's nothing real close around here," he said. "I'll probably be an hour."

Parker said, "If you run into anything I should know, call here."

"You're not going to answer the phone." Lindahl looked startled.

"No, I'm not. But I'll hear what you tell the answering machine."

"Oh. Fine. Good."

Lindahl left, and Parker went back to the kitchen where,

first time through, he'd seen a drawer of tools. First taking the wad of four thousand in new cash from his pocket, he stuffed it deep into the bad-smelling garbage bag under the sink, washed his hands, and turned to the tool drawer. From it he selected a hammer, a Phillips-head screwdriver, a flat-head screwdriver, a hacksaw, and a flashlight. He also took, from the bedroom, a right handed black leather glove. Then he left the converted garage, carrying everything, and walked over to the rear of the boarded-up house.

It was now almost seven in the evening, twilight, just enough illumination left in the sky to see what you were doing. The few houses he could see with lights in their windows looked darker than the rest of the world. No traffic moved out on the road, no sounds could be heard but the small movements of little animals.

Parker stopped at the rear door of the house to study what was here. The door was up two concrete steps from ground level, with filigree iron railings on both sides. A piece of half-inch plywood had been cut to fit between the railings, then screwed to the door frame on both sides and across the top. There were a total of fourteen Phillips-head screws, which would have been put in with a power drill, a tool Lindahl didn't have.

The big question was what length screws they'd used. For half an inch of plywood, a one-inch screw would be plenty, but a guy with a power drill wouldn't mind putting in longer screws, if they were handy.

Parker put on the glove, picked up the Phillips-head screwdriver from the concrete step where he'd laid all the tools, and went to work. The first screw didn't want to budge, having been put in position here a long time ago. Two-handed, he gave it quick hard twists, and at last it unstuck and then turned as smoothly as if it had been oiled.

One-inch; good. Parker pocketed it and went on to the next.

Some of the screws were a little easier, some a little harder, but it all came out to the same; a quarter hour to remove all the screws. Then he pulled the plywood back, to show beyond it an ordinary kitchen door with four windowpanes in its upper half. The doorknob had been removed, because it would have stuck out in the way of the plywood.

The next step was to alter the screws to his own purpose. Turning the sheet of plywood sideways, he leaned it against the front of the railings and put all the screws back in place except for one low on the left side. He turned the screws in only partway, leaving less than a quarter inch of the head still jutting out. He then used the hacksaw to slice off all the screw points back flush to the wood before seating the screws completely into place as before. Now, when the plywood was in position, it would look the same as before, but a simple tug at the top would pull it free.

The screw he hadn't put back he fixed into the upper middle of the plywood on the house side, turning it in only partway, so that it wouldn't show on the outside. From inside the house, that would now be the handle to pull the plywood back into place.

Next was the door. He removed the glove, held it against the pane of glass nearest the missing knob, and hit it with the hammer. The muffled jingle of the breaking glass echoed mostly into the house. Knocking the last couple of shards out of the way, he reached in, found the knob still in place on the inside, turned it, and the door had not been locked; no reason to.

He pushed the door open and stepped in, feet crackling on the broken glass. Turning back, he picked up the plywood and moved it into position, guided by the iron railings that flanked the door. When he pulled the plywood upright against the wall by the screw he'd just added, it fit snugly into place, the shortened screws sliding into the previous holes just enough to hold.

Now the house. The plywood over all the doors and windows made the interior completely black. Switching on the flashlight, Parker saw the house had not been stripped. When the town fathers had sealed it up, they'd still hoped to find a buyer someday, so the plumbing was still here, and the electric fixtures, even the sink and a thirty-year-old refrigerator with its door propped open by a plastic milk box. The electricity and water had been switched off, but that was to be expected.

Parker moved through the dusty empty rooms and found nothing he didn't expect to find. A coating of gray on the floorboards, walls faded to a dull noncolor, long cobwebs in the corners and around the blinded windows. No one had been in here since the plywood had been put up.

Back in the kitchen, he put the flashlight on the counter near the back door; if he had to come back, there wouldn't be time to find some other light source.

There was nothing else here he needed to do or know. He left the house, pulled the door not quite shut, set the sheet of plywood in place, and went back to the converted garage to wait for dinner.

twelve

"We've got a problem tonight," Parker said, "getting to this track of yours."

Lindahl put his beer can down. "What's that?"

They were seated in the living room, eating acceptable pizza, Lindahl drinking beer, Parker water. Outside, full dark had arrived. The silent television set showed sitcoms, so nothing else had happened. In its cage, the parrot seemed mostly asleep, though every once in a while it swiveled its head and made a small gurgling sound and marched a bit in place.

Parker said, "They're looking for two men. They don't know if the two men are still together or if they separated. Once we get where your gun club card doesn't count for anything, when we come to a roadblock and they see two men in the car, they'll want ID from both."

"And you can't show any."

"Nothing useful."

Lindahl thought about that, chewing pizza. "The funny thing is," he said, "once we get to the track, I can help you with ID, but not before."

Parker frowned at him. "Help? How?"

"Every employee carries an encoded ID card," Lindahl told him. "You wear it in a plastic sleeve hangs around your neck. I'm the one bought the machine, I chose it, I know how to use it. I could take your driver's license, photograph it, change the information in the machine, print it out on one of our own laminated blanks. It won't be perfect, but it'll look a lot like the real thing."

"But not till we get there," Parker said.

"If my vehicle had a trunk—"

"No."

"Well, it doesn't, anyway. But the point is, if we can get you there, we can solve your ID problem."

Parker thought about that. He saw what to do, but he didn't like it. Lindahl was so unsure of himself, Parker needed to keep him on a tight leash, but now he couldn't. If Lindahl had time off by himself, would he decide the hell with it, let's call in the cops?

Whatever the odds, Parker would have to risk them. He said, "No, you don't need me there. This machine of yours, it takes mug shots to go on the ID cards, right?"

"Sure."

"There's already a picture on my license. You're going to keep everything the same on it except the name and the home address. You don't need me there to make the change, you only need the license."

Lindahl frowned. "You mean, go there by myself. That way, I'd have to go all the way there twice tonight."

"The second time, I'll drive," Parker said. "It's the only way we can do this, Tom. I can't leave here without identification."

"It's over an hour, each way."

"It's up to you," Parker told him. "We do it this way, or we don't do it. Which do you want?"

Lindahl eyed his beer can. "I'd better switch to coffee," he decided, and got up to go to the kitchen.

thirteen

Lindahl drove off a little before nine. Ten minutes later a knock sounded at the door. Parker was seated in the living room, beside the silent television set, not looking at it, waiting a little longer before going out to explore, but now somebody was here.

Parker waited, not moving. The front door, and the window next to it, were fitted into the original garage door space so sloppily that sound came through from outside, one or two people talking low, somebody scuffing his feet. Then there was a louder, harder knock and a voice called, "Ed! Ed, you in there?" Very aggressive, pushing hard.

Ed? Not looking for Lindahl. No; somebody who had watched and waited for Lindahl to leave, then came over to knock on the door, because it was Ed he wanted to see.

The voice was slightly familiar, recently heard somewhere. Not Thiemann, somebody else.

"Goddammit, Ed, be sociable! Open up this door!" And

whoever it was rattled the doorknob, but since the door wasn't locked, he unexpectedly lurched into the living room, holding the knob to save himself, barking a laugh of surprise and embarrassment.

It was the one-eyed guy with the black patch from the meeting this afternoon at St. Stanislas, and coming in behind him, more cautious and wary, his coat holder, Cory. They both looked at Parker, who stayed in his chair.

The one-eyed man said, "What's the matter, Ed? How come you don't open your door?"

"It's not my door," Parker told him.

"You can answer," the guy insisted. "When somebody comes along, polite, and knocks in a very polite way, and calls out your name, you can answer, can't you?"

"I'm not in a mood for visitors," Parker told him.

The one-eyed man was both surprised and offended. "Not in a mood! You hear that, Cory?"

"Cal," Cory said, a small warning.

But Cal wasn't a man to take warnings. Glaring around the room, he stepped over and dropped backward onto the sofa, facing Parker, saying, "Well, I feel like a visit." Then he blinked with sudden delight and pointed past Parker, crying, "Cory, looka that!"

"It's a parrot," Cory said.

"Goddam, it is a parrot! That's what I oughta have." Leaning toward Parker, gesturing at the patch that covered his left eye, he said, "You can see how that would go with me, can't you?"

"It belongs to Tom," Parker said.

Taking a step forward, Cory said, "Cal doesn't mean he wants it. It just tickled him, that's all. You know, because of the patch."

"I don't want a goddam bird," Cal said, and now he was discontented again. Leaning forward ever closer to Parker, he said, "I bet you don't know we're twins."

"I knew you were brothers," Parker said.

"Yeah, but not twins. It's because of this goddam—" He made an angry swiping gesture toward the patch. "If I could get," he started, then erased that in the air, and sat back, showing himself calm and logical. "The situation is," he said, "if I could get the plastic surgery and the glass eye, I could look just exactly like this handsome fella here."

"The insurance wouldn't pay," Cory explained.

"I wasn't that drunk!" Cal yelled, angry again. "And it was that other sonofabitch's fault, anyway." Leaning forward toward Parker again, now confidential, he said, "All I need's a little money, Ed, you can see that. Where'm I gonna get that kinda money, Ed? I'm a carpenter at the modular home plant over in LeForestville, me and Cory both, where we gonna get fifteen, twenty thousand dollars?"

"I don't know," Parker said.

"I bet you got some money, Ed," Cal said, smiling like he was friendly, showing crooked teeth. "I bet you could help out a fella, if you wanted."

"Quid pro quo," Cory said, to explain things.

So the artist's renderings had done their work, after all, at least with these two. Parker said to Cory, "What's the quo?"

"We don't need to go into all that," Cal said, impatient, sitting back, waving that idea away. "We're just friendly, that's all, a couple friendly guys, helping each other out. Just Cal and Cory Dennison and good old Ed – what was it? Smith?"

"That's right," Parker said.

"Funny kind of name, that, Smith," Cal said, twisting the name to make it sound strange as he winked his good eye at his brother and said, "You don't hear it much. Not around here, you don't."

Parker said, "Get to the point."

"The point?" Cal seemed surprised, as though he'd thought they'd already reached the point. "It's just to be pals, that's all," he said. "Be of, you know, use to each other. Like if we could do something for you. Or like, it should happen, you might have a stash of money around somewhere, you'd probably want to help a friend with this bad fucking eye here."

Parker said, "That's Tom Lindahl's sofa you're sitting on."

Cal grinned and shrugged. "So?"

"Get up from it."

"Oh, I don't think so." Cal spread his arms and legs out, settling into the sofa. "Everybody's gotta be somewhere, you know. Even those—"

"No, they don't," Parker said.

Thrown off, not getting to make his clever remark about how even the missing bank robbers have to be somewhere, wink, wink, Cal blinked his one eye at Parker and said, "What?"

"Some people," Parker said, "don't have to be anywhere." He got to his feet, aware of them both tensing up as they watched him. To Cory, he said, "You're the one with brains. What do you do now?"

"Hey, listen," Cal said.

But Cory patted a hand downward in his brother's direction, looking at Parker as he said, "Maybe we'll talk tomorrow. Maybe with Tom here."

"Ask him," Parker said.

Cory nodded. "We'll do that. Come on, Cal."

Cal looked up at his brother and decided not to argue. He moved to get up, but the sofa, rump-sprung and saggy, was hard to get out of. As he tried to get to his feet while making it look easy, Parker made a small fast gesture with his hands, nothing in particular, but Cal lost his balance and sprawled back onto the sofa.

"You want to be careful," Parker told him.

"Come on, Cal," Cory said, and stuck a hand out, which Cal angrily took, to be hauled up out of the sofa.

They moved toward the still-open door, Parker following, seeing their battered red Dodge Ram out there, with the fitted steel toolbox bolted to the bed. They stepped through, and Parker stood in the doorway behind them. "Always be careful," he told Cal. "You wouldn't want anything to happen to that other eye."

As Cory pulled him toward the pickup with a hand on his elbow, Cal glared back, face distorted, crying, "Never mind the good one! What about this one? What about this one?"

Parker shrugged. "Ask the parrot."

fourteen

Cory drove, so there was no squealing of tires, burning of rubber. Parker watched the Ram go, then stood in the open doorway another five minutes, listening to an absolutely silent night, before he stepped outside, shut the door, and walked down the driveway.

There were two tall streetlights at diagonal corners of the intersection down to his left, but otherwise the road was dark, with here and there the dull gleam of lights inside houses. Parker walked first to his right, past a dark house, then a house where an older couple played some sort of board game in a brightly lit living room, then another dark house, a boarded-up house, and then the last on this side, where a woman muffled up in robes and blankets as though she were on a sleigh in Siberia sat alone to watch TV.

This first walk through the town was simply to get a sense of it, and the sense was of leftovers, of people still in the stadium after the game is done. There were no children watching television, no toys on porches, never more than two people visible in any house. These were the respectable poor, living in retirement in the only place they'd ever known. They wouldn't have much that would be of use to Parker, though there might be one thing. Older not-rich people in an isolated community: Some of them might have handguns.

Down the other side of the road, Parker passed the gas station, closed for the night, with light from a soda machine in front of the office illuminating the pumps and a small night-light gleaming on the wall above the desk inside.

Up till now, there had been no traffic at all through this town at this hour, the blinking signal lights at the intersection controlling nothing. But as he walked just beyond the gas station, Parker did see a car coming this way from the blackness outside the town. He continued to walk, continued to look at the houses, and the car rapidly approached, its high beams becoming troublesome just before the driver dimmed them; which meant he'd seen Parker and was doing the polite thing.

The car slowed, coming into the town, then went on by Parker, who kept walking at a steady pace. A few seconds later he heard the tire-squeal as the car made a U-turn, and here it came again, the opposite way, slowing beside him.

Not a cop. A beat-up older Toyota four-door, some dark color. The passenger window slid down as the car came to a stop beside Parker, and the driver alone in there, a woman, leaned toward him to say, "Can I help you?"

He could keep walking, but she'd just pace him, so he stopped and turned to her. "To do what?" he said.

She didn't seem to know what to do with that answer. She looked younger than the people of this town, probably in her thirties, dashboard-lit in such a way as to give her face harsh angles and extremes of light and shadow. She said, "Are you looking for an address or something?"

"No."

"I just thought— People don't usually walk around here."

"I do."

"But you don't live here."

"I visit here."

"Oh." Now at last on familiar ground, she pasted what was supposed to be a friendly smile on her face and said, "Who are you visiting?"

It would cause less trouble and suspicion just to answer her. "Tom Lindahl."

"Tom! I'm surprised. I thought he was—" Then it occurred to her she might be about to say something insulting about Lindahl, and this might be a friend or relative, so she laughed, an uncomfortable sound, and said, "You know what I mean."

"You thought he was a hermit."

"Yes, I suppose. Yes."

"He is a hermit," Parker said. "But I visit him."

"Well, why not?" she said, moving her hands on the steering wheel as though sorry she'd stopped. "I'm glad he has . . . I'm glad he has visitors."

"And now," Parker said, "I'm doing my after-dinner walk."

"Of course. Well . . ."

She didn't know how to end the encounter, but he did. He nodded and walked on, not looking back. After a long moment of silence back there, the car abruptly burst into life, with another U-turn squeal of tires, and receded quickly into silence.

A few minutes later, nearing the end of his walk-through, he came to the house where the old man had been asleep earlier today on the front porch. Now the only illumination from that house was the fitful blue-gray glitter from a television set, and when Parker looked in the living room window, the same man, in the same clothing, sat asleep straight up on the sofa, the television light playing across him like reflections from a waterfall.

So this was as good a place as any to start. When Parker looked back, the Toyota with the inquisitive woman was gone. He walked around to the back of the house, which from this angle was similar to the boarded-up house he'd entered earlier, including even the concrete steps up to the back door flanked by filigree iron railings.

Taking from his pocket a credit card that had no function any more except what he was going to use it for now, because it had the same burned name on it as the driver's license Lindahl had taken away with him, he slid it down the jamb between frame and door, worked the bolt back from its recess, and pushed the door open. It squeaked, very slightly, but above that he could hear the screams of police sirens and raucous music from the television set at the other end of the house.

This was a smaller structure than the boarded-up house, only one story high, not much larger than Lindahl's converted garage. The messy kitchen was unlit, and so was the small dining room in front of it, crowded with furniture as though the owner had at one point moved here from somewhere larger. A bedroom off the dining room was clearly a seldom-used guest room, so he backtracked to the kitchen, opened a side door there, and found the bedroom.

There were two places people usually kept a handgun inside a house, both in the bedroom: either in a locked box atop a dresser or in a locked drawer in a bedside table. There was no box on top of the dresser in here, only coins, socks, magazines, and a very thin wallet, but the lower of two drawers in the bedside table was locked.

Parker opened the drawer above that one, felt in the near-darkness through a jumble of medicines, flashlight, eyeglasses, and a deck of playing cards, and found the key. He closed that drawer, unlocked the other, and took out a Smith & Wesson Ranger in .22 caliber, a stubby blue-black revolver with a two-inch barrel, moderately accurate across an average room, not much good beyond that. But it would do.

Parker pocketed the revolver, felt some more in the drawer, and found a small heavy cardboard box. When he took it out and opened it, it contained more cartridges. The box was almost full. Had the revolver never been fired? Possibly.

He pocketed both the gun and the box of ammunition, relocked the drawer, and put the key back in the drawer above. To the sounds of forensic explanation from the living room, he silently let himself back out of the house.

As he walked down the side driveway toward the road, the television sound abruptly shut off and lights came on in the living room, spilling out of the windows. Skirting that glow, Parker continued on out to the road, saw the old man just exiting the living room toward the rear of the house, and walked on back to Lindahl's place.

Would any of the people in these houses here have anything else of use to him? No. What he needed was a good amount of cash and clean transportation. He'd start to assemble those once he got the altered driver's license. If he got it.

Back at Lindahl's house, he saw that the answering machine had collected no messages, so possibly Lindahl was simply doing the job. Parker sat down to wait.

Lindahl had said the trip would take a little over an hour each way, and he'd left just before nine, so when the silent television set started the eleven o'clock news, Parker stood, watched the set until he saw there was no fresh news about the bank robbers, then left the house, still with all its lights on, and went over to let himself into the boarded-up house, pulling the plywood panel shut behind him. Using Lindahl's flashlight, he went upstairs, found the pull-down staircase to the attic, and climbed up.

The round window that was the only opening in the house that hadn't been covered with plywood was a pale blur to his right. Switching off the flashlight, he crossed to it and looked out. The window, at the rear of the house, was at head height, about a foot wide. Through it he could see Lindahl's place and a bit of the driveway, but nothing more. Revolver in one pocket and flashlight in the other, he leaned against the wall, looked out the window, and settled down to see what would arrive.

fifteen

At twenty-five after eleven, a glow brightened the front of Lindahl's house, and then his black SUV appeared, moving slowly. It stopped in the usual place, and Lindahl got out, stretched, yawned hugely, and walked over to enter his house.

Parker watched. Nothing else happened over there. Then, after two minutes, the front door opened again and Lindahl stepped out, peering to left and right. He barely glanced at the boarded-up house. He might have called a name, but if he did, Parker couldn't hear it. In any event, after one more look around and a baffled headshake, he went back inside.

Now Parker turned away from the window. The attic was absolutely black, with a rectangular hole somewhere in its floor for the staircase. He took the flashlight from his pocket, closed his fingers over the glass, switched it on, and slowly separated his fingers until he could make out the area ahead of him and the beginning of the staircase.

Going down, he didn't bother to lift the attic stairs into their upper position. Reaching the back door, he switched off the flashlight and put it on the counter, then let himself out, put the plywood in place, and crossed to enter the house.

Lindahl was in the bedroom, but he came out when he heard the front door. The look of bafflement was still on his face. "Where'd you go?"

"Looking around the neighborhood. You did the license?"

Bewilderment was replaced by a proud smile as Lindahl took a laminated card from his shirt pocket and extended it. "Take a look at that."

It looked very good. It was the same New York State driver's license as before, colored in pale pastels, with the same photo of Parker on it, but now his name was William G. Dodd and he lived at 216 N. Sycamore Court, Troy. The card itself seemed to be just slightly thicker than those used by the state of New York, but not enough to attract attention.

"It's good," Parker said, and put the license away in his wallet. "Where'd you get the name and address, make them up?"

"No. Bill Dodd used to work there years ago, before he retired, and that address came off another guy's next of kin on his employment sheet." Shrugging, but pleased with himself, Lindahl said, "I figured we wouldn't want you living too close to the track."

Parker didn't see what difference it made, but let it go, saying, "You want me to drive?"

"God, yes," Lindahl said. "I got stopped three times going down, by the way, and twice coming back. I'm ready to not drive for a while. But just give me five minutes."

"Fine."

Lindahl turned toward the bedroom, then turned back, with a sudden sunny smile on his face. "I'm really going to do it," he said. "Even when I left here, I still wasn't sure, but the minute I saw the place I knew. It's been a weight on me, and now I'm getting rid of it."

"That's good."

"Yes. And it was a good thing we met," Lindahl said. "Good for both of us. Give me five minutes."

part two

one

A billboard ahead on the right read

GRO-MORE RACING
N*ext* R*ight*

"That's the main gate," Lindahl said. "We don't want that. You keep going, about another quarter mile, there's a dirt road on this side."

The dashboard clock read 12:42. In the last hour, William G. Dodd's new driver's license had been inspected by two state troopers at roadblocks and found acceptable; which of course, was more likely at night than by day.

On the drive down, Lindahl had alternated between a kind of buzzing vibrancy, keyed up, giving Parker little spatter-shots of his autobiography, and a deep stillness, as he studied his newly changed interior landscape, as mute as his parrot.

The main gate, when they drove past it, was a broad entry

with parking lots to right and left, a line of entry booths, and the wide hulk of the clubhouse beyond. Large curved iron gates built around stylized outlined shapes of bulls were closed over the entrance. A few dim lights showed here and there in the clubhouse.

Parker said, “Who’s in there now?”

“Two guards. That’s the security office, that light way over to the right. There used to be just one guard at night, but then they found out the guy would usually fall asleep, so now it’s two.”

“Do they patrol? Make rounds?”

“No, they’ve got monitors in the security room, cameras and smoke detectors here and there in the clubhouse and the paddocks, burglar alarms on the ground-floor doors and windows.”

“Are the guards armed?”

“Oh, sure. Handguns in holsters. They’re in uniform, they work for a security company, that part is all contracted out. Here’s where we turn.”

The turn was a narrow dirt road unmarked except for a Dead End sign. Parker drove slowly, trying to see into the darkness to his right where the track would be. “Is that a wall?”

“Wooden wall, eight foot high, runs the whole perimeter. This road is used to bring horses in and out, supplies, ambulance when they need one. Up ahead here, turn right to the gate.”

"Can they see these headlights?"

"No, there's nobody around in there except the guards in the security office. Those other lights are just for the fire code."

This gate was plain chain-link, eight feet high like the wall stretching away to left and right. Parker stopped just before it, the headlights shining through the chain-link fence onto the white clapboard end wall of the clubhouse. Tall white wooden fences angled out from the corners of the clubhouse at front and back, curved to meet the perimeter wall at some distance to both sides, making a large enclosed area, part blacktop, part dirt. A number of trucks and pickups and horse vans were parked along the wall to the left, with an ambulance and a fire engine along the wall to the right.

Opening his door, Lindahl said, "I'll turn off the alarm, then I can unlock the gate."

"Isn't there a security camera along here?"

"No," Lindahl said. "They only watch the inside and the paddocks. They're not worried so much about break-ins as fire. Or somebody wanting to hurt the horses. I'll be a minute."

Parker waited as Lindahl opened a metal box beside the gate, punched numbers onto the pad in there, then took a full ring of keys from his pocket, selected one, and opened the padlock securing the gate. He opened it wide, then gestured for Parker to follow him. He walked confidently in the headlight glare toward the clubhouse, then turned to wave to Parker to stop in front of more chain-link fence, this making a kind of three-sided cage extending out from the middle of the clubhouse wall.

Coming around to the driver's door, Lindahl said, "Leave the engine and lights on a minute, I want you to see this."

Parker got out of the Ford and went with Lindahl to the fence. The outer side of it was another gate, and inside, a concrete ramp sloped down to a basement level, then went straight under the building, stopping at a featureless metal garage door tucked back about eight feet.

"Inside there," Lindahl said, "is the corridor, with the safe room on the left. The armored car backs down, they open the door, and they load on the boxes. Food deliveries go down there, too, and all kinds of supplies. But we have to get in a different way now, so you can turn the car off and we'll go in that door over there."

The door was near the front corner of the clubhouse, solid wood with No Admittance stenciled on it. By the time Parker had left the Ford and walked over, Lindahl had this door, too, unlocked. "There's no cameras until we come to the main corridor," he said.

Parker said, "I'd expect more security."

"Well, it's a small track out in the country," Lindahl said as he led the way down the dim-lit narrow corridor past closed doors. "It has two twenty-four-day meets, spring and fall, and it's shut down the rest of the time. They've been wanting to sign on to a tote-board system so they could be open for betting at other tracks the rest of the year, but so far it hasn't worked out. I think the population around here is too small. So the track never makes a whole lot of money, and there's never once been a break-in in all these years. A couple times crazies tried to get at the horses, but nothing else. We go through here, it bypasses the main corridor."

Lindahl opened a door on the left, and they entered a broad low-ceilinged room with eight desks neatly spaced on a black linoleum floor. A fluorescent halo around a large wall clock gave illumination. Most of the desks were covered with papers and other items, including a leftover bacon and omelet breakfast on a green plastic plate.

"This is where the accounts are kept," Lindahl said, and pointed. "My office used to be— Damn!"

He had bumped into the wrong desk, causing the breakfast to flip over and hit the floor facedown. Lindahl stooped to pick up the plate, but the omelet stuck to the black linoleum, which was now a black ocean, and that omelet the sandy desert island, with the solitary strip of bacon sticking up from it, slightly slumped but brave, the perfect representation of the stranded sailor, alone and waiting for his cartoon caption. On the floor, it looked like what the Greeks call acheiropoietoi, a pictorial image not made by a human hand.

"I ought to clean that up," Lindahl said, frowning down doubtfully at the new island.

"A mouse did it," Parker told him. "Drop the plate on it and let's go."

"Fine."

Lindahl led the way across the room and out another door to another corridor that looked identical to the first. They went leftward, Lindahl still leading the way, Parker making sure to remember the route.

Lindahl stopped where the corridor made a right turn into a wider hallway. Pausing, he leaned to glance around the corner, then said, "Take a look. See the camera?"

Parker leaned forward. Some distance down the hall, on the opposite side, was a closed door with a small pebble-glass window and a pushbar. Mounted on the wall above the door was a light, aimed downward, flooding the immediate area and giving some illumination down as far as the end here. Above the light, just under the dropped ceiling, a camera was mounted on a small metal arm. The camera was at this moment pointed toward the other end of the hall but was moving, turning leftward toward the wall. As Parker watched, it stopped, hesitated, and began to turn back in the other direction.

Parker leaned back. "Tell me about it."

"It does a one-minute sweep, back and forth. Once it comes back in this direction and starts the other way, it looks down here for just a few seconds. After that, we have forty seconds to walk down the hall and through the door. That's the stairwell; no cameras. We go down in the basement. Here it comes."

Lindahl waited, seeming to count seconds in his head, then looked around the corner and said, "Good."

They strode down the hall, the camera continuing to turn away from them. Lindahl pushed open the door, and Parker followed him through, to a stairwell of concrete flights of steps leading up and down. A small light mounted on the wall above the door illuminated this section of stairs.

They went downstairs one flight to the bottom of the stairwell, where an identical door had an identical light over it. Lindahl said, "This is a little tricky, because if I open the door when the camera's faced straight across the hall, the guards might see the light change on their screen, so hold on."

He bent down to the small window, cheek against the glass and head angled back as he squinted up and out. "I can just see it when— Oh, good. Right now."

He opened the door and immediately walked briskly to the right. Parker followed. The end of the hall down here was very close, closer than upstairs, with a metal fire door in it. As he walked, Lindahl chose another key from his ring, quickly unlocked the end door, and stepped through. Following him, Parker looked back and saw the camera still turning away.

Once this door was closed, the space they were in was

completely without light. "I don't want to turn the light on in here," Lindahl said, "because the camera might see it, around the door edges, I don't know for sure. Hold on."

Parker waited, leaning against the closed door. He heard Lindahl shuffle away, then sounds of a key in a lock and a door opening, and then lights went on, ceiling fluorescents, in a room on the right.

Lightspill showed him the space he was in. Empty, and longer than wide, it had a concrete floor, concrete-block walls, and a windowless metal garage door at the far end, certainly the same one he'd seen from outside.

A forklift truck stood in the near right corner. When Parker moved to the room Lindahl had illuminated, the doorway was a little taller and wider than average, to accommodate the forklift. Lindahl was now fastening the gray metal fireproof door to a hook in the concrete floor, to keep it open.

This would be the safe room, a windowless square low-ceilinged space in concrete block painted a flat gray. To the left, half a dozen smallish oblong metal boxes stood on a mover's pallet. Each box was marked with the logo Gro-More Racing in white letters on its long sides. Metal shelves on the right contained more of the boxes plus the kind of sectioned tray inserted into cash register drawers, and a toolkit and some miscellaneous supplies.

Lindahl said, "You see the setup."

"Yes."

"The track owns the boxes, so the empties always come back here. Every once in a while, one gets dented or the hinges warp, and they throw it out. They're careful, they put them inside black plastic bags in the Dumpster."

"But you know how it works," Parker said. "So you've been taking them home."

"I have seven." Lindahl's pride in his accomplishment immediately gave way to self-disgust. "I was brilliant," he said. "I worked it all out, every damn thing but coming down here and actually doing the deed."

Parker said, "You figured to move that stuff in your Ford?"

"No, that wouldn't work, I know that much." Lindahl shrugged. "For that, I need a little truck, like a delivery truck."

"Do you have one of those?"

"No, I'd rent it." Then Lindahl grinned at Parker, almost defiantly, and said, "Yeah, I know, just one more thing to tell the police I'm the one did it. But I don't care if they know, I'm long gone. I'd even leave the truck and the empty boxes at my place, because I won't be coming back."

That was true. Parker said, "Anything else to show me?"

"No, this is it, only we've got to go back out the way we came in. If you open that door to the ramp from outside, it flashes a light in security. You have to switch off the alarm on this side, and then open it. And then, if you close it and don't re-alarm it, the light in security goes on, anyway. So when we do it, next Saturday, if we do it – well, when we do it, we have to go in and out the same way, drive the truck out, come back in, lock up, switch the alarm on, walk around and up the stairs and out. Anything else you want to see?"

Parker pointed at the metal boxes on the pallet. "They locked?"

"No need."

"Open one."

"Sure."

The lids were two long flat metal pieces, accordion-hinged to the long sides of the boxes. Lindahl went to one knee in front of the pallet and lifted open the two parts of the lid, which was apparently pretty heavy. Inside, cashier drawer inserts like the ones on the shelves were stacked, it looked like three deep, but these were full of cash; paper money sorted into compartments from the left, coins to the right.

"These things really weigh," Lindahl said as he closed the lid and got to his feet.

"They look it."

"Anything else?"

"How much is in there, usually, on a Saturday night?"

"Probably more than a hundred thousand, less than one-fifty."

Parker nodded. Enough to keep him moving.

Lindahl, proud and anxious, said, "So what do you think?"

"It looks good."

With a huge relieved smile, Lindahl said, “I knew you’d see it. You ready to go?”

“Yes.”

On their way out, up the stairs from the basement, Lindahl said, “You know, I know why you wanted me to open that box. You didn’t want your fingerprints on it.”

“That’s right,” Parker said.

two

Parker didn't speak until they were well away from the track, headed north, and then he said, "If we're going to do this, you'll have to do what I say."

"You're the pro, you mean."

"I care whether I get arrested or not."

"Oh, I care," Lindahl said. "Don't get me wrong, I don't have some kind of death wish over here. If those bastards catch me and put me in jail, they've beat me again. I don't want that. I'm not going to jail, trust me, that's not going to happen."

"You'd rather die first."

Lindahl grimaced, trying to work out an answer to that, and finally said, "Would you give up?"

"I don't want them on my tail," Parker said. "That's the point."

"They were on your tail. When I first saw you, they were right down the hill behind you."

"It's fresh in my memory," Parker assured him. "That's why, if we go ahead and do it, we do it my way, and you don't argue."

"But I can say no, I guess," Lindahl said. "I can say no, I don't want to do that, and then we don't do it. Like if you say, 'Now we go kill the two guys in security,' I can say no, and we don't do it."

"I'm not out to kill anybody," Parker said. "It only makes the heat worse."

"Well, whatever it might be," Lindahl said. "If I don't like it, I can say no, and we don't do it."

"You're right," Parker told him. "You can always say no."

"Good. We understand each other." Lindahl nodded at the windshield. "Lights out there."

They had met only the occasional other moving car, this time of night, but up the road ahead of them now were the unmistakable lights of another roadblock. Those roadblocks would be in position all night tonight, and maybe tomorrow night, too.

The law was looking for two men, possibly separate but possibly together, so any car out late at night with two men in it attracted their interest. Also, with so little traffic out here on the rural roads in the middle of the night, the guys on duty were getting bored. For the first time, Parker and Lindahl were asked to step out of the Ford while the troopers did a quick flashlight scan of the interior. They weren't patted down, though, and once again Parker's new license was accepted without question.

They were the only car at the roadblock, and when they left it, driving north into darkness, that cluster of lights in the rearview mirror was still the only illumination to be seen. Lindahl kept twisting around to look back at those lights, and it wasn't until they disappeared that he spoke again. "I guess you have an idea of what to do. About the track, I mean."

"Yes."

"I think it must be different from mine."

"Parts of it."

"Which parts?"

"In the first place," Parker said, "we don't take those metal boxes with us. There's no reason to lug all that weight around."

"The money's gotta be in something."

"Is there a mall around where you are? Someplace open on Sunday?"

"About forty miles away," Lindahl said, "over toward Albany."

"Tomorrow," Parker told him, "you drive over there. Get two duffel bags. You know what I mean, big canvas bags."

"Like the army uses."

"That's right."

Lindahl shook his head. "I don't know," he said. "You saw how much money was there."

"All we want is the big bills," Parker told him. "Nothing under a ten. And no change."

“Oh.” Nodding slowly, Lindahl said, “I guess that makes sense.”

“And also get two pairs of plastic kitchen gloves.”

“For fingerprints; fine. Anything else?”

“No, that’s all we’ll need. And fill the gas tank, it’s getting low.”

“Sure.” Lindahl was quiet for a minute, but then he frowned and said, “Why do I have to do all this tomorrow? There’s closer places I can go to on Monday.”

“Because we’re taking the money tomorrow night,” Parker said.

three

"No!" Lindahl was deeply shocked. "That's no good! We won't have any time at all to get away!"

"In the first place," Parker said, "let's get rid of that thirty-six-hour fantasy of yours. You can't go on the run, because you can't hide. Where do you figure to be, thirty-six hours later? Oregon? Where do you sleep? Do you go to a motel and pay with cash? A credit card places you, and the law by then is watching your accounts. So do you pay cash? The motel wants your license plate number. Oh, from New York State?"

"Jesus."

"Anywhere you go in this country, everybody's on the same computer. It doesn't matter if you're across the street or across the country, as soon as you make any move at all, they know where you are. You gonna try to leave the country? You got a passport?"

"No," Lindahl said. He sounded subdued. "I've never traveled much."

"Not a good time to start," Parker told him. "You can't run away, you don't know those ropes. So instead of being the guy that did it and you're thumbing your nose and they'll never get you, you're the guy that didn't do it, and you're staying right there where you always were, and sure, let them go ahead and search, and you were home in bed last night same as any other night, and you don't spend any of that cash for a year. You want to pull the job and not do time for it? That's how."

"That's all . . ." Lindahl shook his head, gestured vaguely in the air in front of himself, like someone trying to describe an elephant to a person who'd never seen one. "That's different from what I had in mind. That isn't the same thing."

"You want two things," Parker reminded him. "Or so you said. You want revenge. And you want the money."

"Well," Lindahl said, and now he seemed a little embarrassed, a little sheepish, "I kind of wanted them to know."

"Because you were gonna disappear."

"But you say I can't do that."

Parker said, "You aren't used to the life on the other side of the law. There's too many things you don't know, too many mistakes you can make. You can have your money, and you can have your revenge, and maybe even a couple of your old bosses think you maybe did it, but they can't prove it, and you and your parrot just go on living the way you did before."

"That's not what I had in mind," Lindahl said again. "What I had in mind was, I don't live like this any more. I don't shoot rabbits for my dinner. I don't curl up in that crappy little house and never see anybody and everybody knows I'm that crazy hermit and nobody gives a shit about me."

"You did it for four years," Parker reminded him. "You can do it one year more. A little less. Next July, you tell a few people you're going on vacation, you're driving somewhere. Then you take the money and you go wherever you want to go—"

"Someplace warm."

"That's up to you. When you get there, you start a checking account, you put a couple grand of your cash in it every few weeks, you rent a place to live, you drive back up here, pack your stuff, tell whoever you're paying your rent to that you decided to retire someplace warm, and there you are."

Lindahl was quiet for a long while as Parker drove, the headlights pushing that fan of pale white out ahead of them, moving through hilly countryside, sleeping towns, here and there a night-light but mostly as dark as when the continent was empty.

Finally, with a long sigh, Lindahl said, "I think I could do that."

"I think so, too."

"It's like hunting, I see that. In some ways, it's like

hunting. The main thing you have to be is patient. If you're patient, you'll get what you want."

"That's right."

"I'd have to— If that's what we do, I'd have to hide the money. I mean, really well, where they wouldn't find it. Where nobody would find it."

"I'll show you where," Parker said.

Surprised, Lindahl said, "You already know a place?"

"But the other thing you've got to do," Parker told him, "is get rid of those metal bank boxes. You don't need them, and you don't want any lawman to come across them, because you don't have any answers to those questions."

"You're right," Lindahl said. "I didn't think about them. They're just in the furnace room, stacked in the corner."

"Wipe your fingerprints off."

"They're still in the black plastic bags, from when they were thrown away in the Dumpster. I just left them that way."

"That's good. Take them with you tomorrow, find another Dumpster, maybe at this mall you're going to, get rid of them in a way that they won't come back."

"All right, I can do that." Curious, half turning in his seat, Lindahl said, "You really know where to hide the money?"

"In the boarded-up house in front of you."

"Oh, I don't know," Lindahl said. "I don't think it'd be easy to get in there. Not without making a mess."

"I've already been inside," Parker told him. "It's all set up. I'll show you tomorrow."

"You've been in there? My God."

"In case it would turn out to be a bad idea to be in your house," Parker said.

"I'll have to see this."

Parker said nothing to that, and they drove in silence another while. It was well after four in the morning by now, and it would be after five before they got where they were going. And then Lindahl had a lot to do tomorrow.

"You know," Lindahl said about fifteen minutes later, "now it is real. When I first went back to the track, and looked at it, and realized I was still goddam mad about what happened and still wanted to get back at them, I thought then it was finally real, but it wasn't. It was still my fantasy, riding off into the west like somebody in the movies. Like Fred Thiemann saying we were a posse, only without the horses. That was his fantasy, and it sure bit him on the ass, didn't it?"

"Yes," Parker said.

"And my fantasy would have done the same thing. So now, for the first time, it really is real."

Lindahl looked out at the darkness and smiled. Parker didn't tell him anything.

four

When they drove past the boarded-up house, coming into Pooley at last, Lindahl frowned at it and said, "You really got in there."

"We'll look at it tomorrow," Parker said. "We both need sleep."

It was nearly five-thirty in the morning, false dawn smudging the sky up to their right, suggesting the silhouettes of hills. The only lights showing in the town were down at the intersection, the streetlight and blinker signal and night-lights of the gas station.

Lindahl parked in his usual place and got out of the car, yawning. Parker, getting out on the other side, paused to listen. Not a sound anywhere. He followed Lindahl inside, where at first the television set was the only light source, but then Lindahl switched on a floor lamp beside the sofa, switched off the television, and said, "That sofa isn't bad. I'll get you a pillowcase and a blanket."

“You got an alarm clock?”

“Sure. What time should I set it?”

“Ten.”

Surprised, Lindahl said, “That doesn’t give us much sleep.”

“You’ll sleep when we’re finished,” Parker promised him.

five

Lindahl kept yawning as they walked over to the boarded-up house. It was ten-thirty in the morning, and they'd been up half an hour, finishing a silent breakfast before coming out here to cold damp air, the sky a grayish white as though starting to mildew. Parker led the way to the rear door of the house, where he reached up to the top of the plywood and pulled it back.

"Uh!" Lindahl broke off in midyawn, staring in astonishment. "Was that always like that?"

"I fixed it yesterday."

Lindahl came closer to study the plywood, touching a finger to the stubby end of a sawed-off screw. "You cut them back."

"Right."

"And what's that one in the middle for?"

"To pull it closed when you're inside. Come on."

Parker pushed open the door and motioned for Lindahl to

precede him. As he then stepped in and maneuvered the plywood back into place, Lindahl said, "Is that my flashlight?"

"Yes. We'll need it. In fact, turn it on now."

Lindahl did, and Parker closed them in, then said, "Give me the light, I've been through here before."

"Fine."

They went up through the black house to the attic, and Lindahl went over to look out the unblocked window. "This is where you were when I got back last night," he said. "In case I brought the police or something."

"That's right." Parker pointed the flashlight to the area behind the stairwell, where the roof angled down closest to the floor, leaving only a three-foot height of wall. Discarded there were a bent old cardboard suitcase and some rolls of curtains and curtain rods. "You put your duffel bag in with that stuff, and you leave it there until you go to your someplace warm. And once it's there, you put a couple full-length screws in the plywood, just in case anybody ever comes around to be sure everything's sealed solid."

"And I'll rub a little dirt on them."

"Good."

They went back downstairs and out, and while Parker put the plywood in place, he said, "I'll come along with you to this mall, see if there's anything I need. Let's go put those money boxes into your van."

"All right."

*

Parker put the pistol in his jacket pocket before they left. He had to drive again, because Lindahl was feeling the effects of four hours' sleep. The seven metal boxes in their sheaths of black plastic filled the rear seat so high Parker could only use the outside mirrors.

The first police blockade they came to was manned by the same sour older trooper as yesterday. "I saw you two before," he said as Parker handed over his new license.

"Untrained men with guns," Parker reminded him. "Hickory Rod and Gun. No guns today, though."

"At least nobody got killed yesterday," the trooper said, giving him back the license.

"Any more word on those two guys?"

"Not a peep." His total disaffection dragged the trooper's face down like a double dose of gravity. "You ask me," he said, "those two are on the beach in Florida this very minute. But nobody asked me."

"See if your boss will send you down there to look for them," Parker suggested.

"You can move along now," the trooper said.

They drove on, and Lindahl said, "You don't get nervous, do you?"

"Nothing to get nervous about. Keep an eye out for someplace to get rid of these boxes."

That was twenty miles farther on, a demolition site where an old bowling alley was being torn down, the two Dumpsters already half full of a great miscellany of stuff, the site empty and unguarded on a Sunday morning. They transferred the seven money boxes, dividing them into both Dumpsters to make them a little less of a presence, then drove on to the mall, a smaller older place with only one of its two anchor stores still up and running. The shops down the line between the living major retailer and the dead one made an anthology of national brand names. The parking area was a quarter full, so they could leave the car very close to the entrance, just beyond the empty handi-capped spaces.

They went inside, and Parker said, "You go ahead. You want two duffel bags and two pairs of plastic gloves. I'm gonna look around, and I'll meet you on the way out."

"Okay."

Lindahl took a shopping cart and pushed it away into the sparsely populated store. Parker watched him go, then turned and walked back outside and headed down the row of secondary shops. On the way in, he'd picked the one he thought he probably wanted, a youth clothing store featuring baggy jeans and baseball caps and sweatshirts with penitentiary names on them.

Yes. Reaching that store, looking in the plate-glass window past the display of elaborate sneakers designed like space stations, he saw no customers, only the clerk, a skinny high school kid wearing the store's product as he moved slowly around, halfheartedly neatening the stock.

Parker went into the store, and the kid looked up, first

hopeful and then blank when he realized this was unlikely to be a customer. "Yes, sir? What can I do for you?"

"Well," Parker said, and showed him the pistol, "you can open that cash register over there and then you can lie face-down on the floor behind the counter."

The kid gaped at the pistol and then at Parker, as though he'd lost the ability to understand English. Parker lifted the gun so it pointed at the kid's nose from a foot away. "Or," he said, "I can shoot you in the face and open the cash register myself."

"No, I'll do it!"

The kid abruptly moved, all jangly limbs, bumping into things as he hurried around the end of the counter and opened the cash register. He stepped back from it and stared at Parker. "You won't shoot me?"

"Not if you're facedown on the floor."

The kid dropped as though in fact he had been shot, and when he was on the floor, he put his hands over the back of his head, trembling fingers entwined.

Parker reached over the counter into the cash register drawer and removed the twenties and tens, touching only the money. Then he looked down at the kid and said, "Look at your watch."

The enlaced hands sprang apart, and the kid arched his back to look at the large round watch on his left wrist.

"I'll be outside for five minutes. If I look through the window and see you up, I'll shoot. Five minutes. Got that?"

"Yes, sir." The kid kept staring at the watch, body arched.

Parker turned away, left the shop, and walked back to the large store, where he went inside and found Lindahl on line at a checkout counter, only one other shopper in front of him. In his shopping cart were two dark brown duffel bags folded into clear plastic bags and two pairs of yellow kitchen gloves mounted on cardboard in shrink-wrap. He nodded to Parker: "Found it. You get anything?"

"No, I just looked around."

Lindahl's turn came, and he paid and got his purchases in a large plastic bag with the store's name over a smiley face. They walked out of the store, Lindahl carrying the bag and saying, "Should I drive back?"

"Sure."

Parker gave him the keys. In the car, they started out to the road, but then had to wait while a police car rushed by, lights flashing and siren ablare. Lindahl watched them go by, startled. "What do you think that is?"

"Nothing to do with us," Parker said.

six

They stopped at a run-down traditional diner for lunch on the way back. They chose a table beside the large window with its view out to very little Sunday traffic on this secondary road, and after they'd given the waitress their orders, Parker said, "Tell me about the Dennisons."

"The who? Oh, Cory and Cal? What do you want to know about them for?"

"They came to see me last night. Right after you left."

"They came— They were at my place?"

"They think I might be one of the missing robbers."

"Jesus!" Lindahl looked as though he just might jump straight up and out of the diner and run a hundred miles down the road. "What are they gonna do?"

"If I am one of the robbers," Parker said, "they think I must have a bunch of money on me."

"But you don't."

"But if I was and I did, I could give Cal money to get plastic surgery and an artificial eye."

"Oh, for—" No longer in a panic, Lindahl now looked as though he'd never heard anything so dumb. "They said that to you? You're the robber, and give us some of the money?"

"The robber part wasn't said."

"But that's what it was all about. And if you give them the money, they won't report you? Is that the idea?"

"I suppose so."

"That's a Cal idea, all right," Lindahl said. "He's jumped off barn roofs since he was a little kid."

"Cory's the smart one," Parker agreed, "but he follows the other one's lead. They say they're gonna come back today and talk to you."

Lindahl was astonished all over again. "Talk to me? About what?"

"Am I really your old friend Ed Smith."

Lindahl leaned back in the booth and spread his hands. "Well, you really are my old friend Ed Smith. I oughta know who you are."

"That's right," Parker said. As the waitress brought their plates, he said, "Over lunch, we'll work out the details of that. In case somebody talks to you and then talks to me."

"Good. We'll do that."

"We've only got to worry about today," Parker said, "and then we're done with it."

With a surprised laugh, Lindahl said, "That's right! Just today and tonight. The whole thing, it's almost over."

seven

They got back to Lindahl's house a little before two. The vehicle parked in front of it was not the Dennisons' Dodge Ram, but a black Taurus that Parker recognized as Fred Thiemann's. Then its driver's door opened, and a woman in her fifties climbed out, dressed in jeans and a windbreaker. She must have been waiting for them to get back.

Parker said, "The wife?"

"Jane," Lindahl said, and looked worried. "What's gone wrong?"

"She'll tell us."

Lindahl parked next to the Taurus as Jane Thiemann went over to stand by the door to the house, waiting for them, frowning. Looking at her through the windshield, Parker saw a woman who was weighed down by something. Not angry, not frightened, but distracted enough not to care what kind of appearance she made. She was simply out in the world, braced for whatever the bad news would turn out to be.

Parker and Lindahl got out of the SUV, and Lindahl said, “Jane. How’s Fred?”

“Coming apart at the seams.” She turned bleak eyes toward Parker. “You’re Ed Smith, I guess.”

“That’s right.”

“Fred’s afraid of you,” she said. “I’m not sure why.”

Parker shrugged. “Neither am I.”

Lindahl said, “You want to come in?”

“Fred sent me for his rifle.”

“Oh, sure. I have it locked in the rack in the bedroom. Come on in.”

They stepped into the living room, and the parrot bent its head at Jane Thiemann in deep interest. She looked at the television set. “You keep that on all the time?”

“It’s something moving. I’ll be right back.”

Lindahl went into the bedroom, and Parker said, “What was the urgency? Fred doesn't figure to use it, does he?"

She gave him a sharp look. “On himself, you mean?”

“On anything. He isn’t hunting deer today.”

Coming back from the bedroom, carrying Thiemann’s rifle, Lindahl said, “Deer season doesn’t start till next month.”

She looked at her husband’s rifle as Lindahl offered it to her at port arms, and said, “I’d like to sit down a minute.”

“Well, sure,” he said, surprised and embarrassed. As she

dropped onto the sofa, not sitting, but dropping as though her strings had been cut, he stepped back and leaned the rifle against the wall. “I’m sorry, Jane, I forget how to be civilized. You want something to drink? Water? I think I got Coke.”

Parker said, “You want the television off?”

“Yes, please,” she said, and to Lindahl said, “I’d like some water, if I could.”

Lindahl left the room, and Parker switched off the set, then sat in the chair beside it, facing the sofa. He said, “Fred’s in shock.”

“We’re both in shock,” she said. “But he’s in more than shock. He’s angry, and he’s scared, and he feels like he’s got to do something, but he doesn’t know what. Thanks, Tom.”

Lindahl, having returned to give her a glass of water with ice cubes in it, now stood awkwardly for a second, uncomfortable about taking the seat on the sofa next to her. He dragged over a wooden kitchen chair from the corner and sat on that, midway between Parker and Jane Thiemann.

Parker said, “What does he say, mostly?”

“All kinds of things. A lot about you.”

“Me?”

“He doesn’t understand you, and he feels that he has to, somehow. The only thing he knows for sure, if it wasn’t for you, this would all be different now.”

“That fella would still be dead.”

"Oh, I know that, we both know that, he isn't blaming you, he's blaming what he calls 'my own stupid self.' But if it had been just him and Tom up there, they would have gone to the troopers, and who knows what would have happened?"

"Nothing good," Parker said.

"Well, maybe." She drank some of the water, then sat holding the glass in both hands in her lap. "Or maybe they would have seen it was an accident," she said, "and that man was . . . he was only . . . wouldn't have relatives or—"

"Garbage," Parker said. "A man, but garbage."

"It's harsh when you say it that way," she said, "but yes. The troopers might have looked at it, might have seen what Fred was and what that other man was, and just said, 'Well, it was an accident, we won't make a big deal out of it.' Of course, now he can't do that."

"He never could," Parker said. "That fella has an identity. They'll find it, from fingerprints or DNA or dental records or something else. He'll have relatives, they'll want to be satisfied. Knowing their cousin is drinking himself to death is one thing; knowing he's been shot in the back is something else."

"Oh!"

"Fred wouldn't be hit with a whole lot," Parker told her, "but he would do some time inside."

"That's what scared him," she said, and now she did look as though she might cry, but shook her head and kept talking. "One of the things that scared him. The idea of . . . prison . . . we can't . . . we have our own—"

"Tom told me," Parker said. "Afterward, he told me. He had to."

"I haven't blabbed around to anyone else, Jane," Lindahl said. "Honest to God."

"Oh, I believe you." With that bleak look at Parker again, she said, "That whole thing hit Fred worse even than it did George. He's had to take pills to sleep, or he just lies there all night, thinking about that cell, imagining that cell. He's in the cell more than George is."

Parker said, "How long is George in for?"

"Oh, a year more, at the most," she said, dismissing it. "At the most. It was post-stress syndrome, everybody knows that's what it was. His army record couldn't have been better, everybody says so. Did Tom tell you he was wounded?"

"No."

"I wasn't telling stories, Jane," Lindahl said.

"I understand that." To Parker she said, "He was wounded, too. A roadside bomb." She slid her palm down over her left hip. "It burned a lot of skin off there and smashed a joint. He's got a plastic joint in there."

"So they'll let him out," Parker said, "as soon as they can."

"No more than a year."

Parker nodded. "Have you mentioned to Fred, George will want to see him when he gets out?"

She blinked at him. "Well, he knows— What do you mean?"

Nodding at the rifle against the wall, Parker said, "He's in pain right now. He might decide that thing's better than a sleeping pill."

Her eyes widened, and a trembling hand moved up toward her face, but she didn't speak. She'd known the same truth but had been trying not to think it.

Parker said, "When you take the rifle back to him, remind him, George will be very disappointed, all he's been through, if his father isn't there to say hello when he gets out."

"I will," she said. "That might . . ." She looked around the room. "I don't need any more water."

Lindahl jumped up to take the glass from her. "We're sorry, Jane," he said. "None of us wanted this to happen."

"It isn't you two, it's him. That's the worst of it, he knows it's him." She got to her feet, slightly unsteady. "I shouldn't be away from there too long."

Parker stood and told her, "With you on hand, he'll come through this."

"I hope you're right."

Lindahl handed her the rifle. "The safety's on."

"Good." She staggered slightly under the unaccustomed weight, which meant her husband hadn't introduced her to hunting. "I'll tell Fred what you said," she told Parker. "About George wanting him there, when he comes back."

"Good."

"I'll walk you out," Lindahl said, and did so. Parker waited, and then Lindahl came back in to say, "You were very sympathetic." He sounded surprised. "I didn't think you'd have that kind of sympathetic manner."

"I had to," Parker said. "You know Thiemann's thinking about killing himself. If he does, the cops'll talk to the wife three minutes before they find out what happened, and ten minutes after that, they're right at this door." Parker shook his head. "I'll be as sympathetic as I have to. Neither of us wants a gun battle with the law."

eight

Three minutes after Jane Thiemann left, the door opened and Cal Dennison sauntered in, saying, "That lady had a gun."

"She's looking for the bank robbers," Parker said.

As Cory entered, shutting the door behind himself as he nodded a cautious greeting toward Lindahl, Cal laughed and said, "Well, I bet she come to the right place."

"No, the wrong place," Parker said.

Lindahl said, "Cal, you're jumping off half-assed again."

"Oh, I don't think so," Cal said, and pulled a much-crumpled sheet of paper from his pocket. Smoothing it as best he could on his dark gray shirtfront, he held it out toward Lindahl and said, "You tell me, Tom. You just go right ahead."

Lindahl, not touching it, reluctantly looked at the now familiar artist's rendering and grudgingly said, "Well, they look a little alike, I can see how they're a little alike."

"A little alike?" Cal swung to hold the paper out with both hands at its side edges, arms straight out as he aimed the picture at Parker and said, "Whadaya say, Ed? If you saw this fella comin down the road toward you, would you say, 'Looks like I got a long-lost twin brother,' or what?"

"He could be a thousand guys," Parker said.

"Not a thousand."

Lindahl said, "Cal, if this picture looks so much like Ed here, and everybody up at the meeting at St. Stanislas had a copy of the picture, and Ed was standing right there with us, how come nobody else saw it? How come everybody in the goddam parking lot didn't turn around and make a citizen's arrest?"

"It was that story in school," Cal said, and frowned deeply as he turned to hand the sketch to Cory. "That writer we had to read, all that spooky stuff. Poe. The something letter. All about how everybody's looking for this letter, and nobody can find it, and that's because it's right out there in plain sight, the one place you wouldn't think it would be. So here's a fella, and a whole bunch of guys get together to find him, and where's the best place he oughta hide? Right with the bunch looking for him, the one place nobody in the county's gonna think to look."

Voice arched with sarcasm, Lindahl said, "And you, Cal, you're the only one there figured it out."

"Could happen," Cal said, comfortable with himself. "Could happen."

"Not this time," Parker said, and Cory said, "Look at that."

They all turned to the television set, and there was the artist's rendering again, this time with superimposed red letters: FUGITIVE BANDIT STRIKES AGAIN.

"Jesus!" Cal said. "Where's the goddam sound on that thing?"

Lindahl stepped quickly over to the remote on top of the set and brought the sound on, an off-camera female voice saying, "—possibly still working together." The picture on the screen switched from the artist's rendering to a wide shot of the shopping mall where Parker and Lindahl had been this morning. "It was a slow morning at The Rad in Willoughby Hills Center until the bandit—or bandits—put in their appearance."

As the television picture cut to the exterior of the clothing store Parker had robbed, showing uniformed police going in and out of the place, Parker was aware of Lindahl vibrating beside him, shock and anger working their way through him but so far not erupting into speech. Parker's hand went into his right trouser pocket, lightly touching the pistol there. It would have to be all three of them, if it started now.

"Clerk Edwin Kislamski was alone in the shop at eleven-forty-five this morning when a man entered, threatened Mr. Kislamski with a handgun, and robbed the cash register of over three thousand dollars."

The clerk himself now appeared, seated on a wooden bench against a green wall in what looked like the front room of a state police barracks. For some reason, he was wrapped in a thick cream blanket, as though he were a near-drowning victim. He clutched the blanket to himself with both hands. Above it, a kind of terrified half-smile flickered across his face like distant searchlights as he spoke: "I recognized him right away." An apparent cut, and then, "Oh, yeah, I got a real good look at him. I got a better look at him than I wanted."

"Hah!" Cal crowed. "I bet that's true! Change your pants, sonny!"

"Shut up, Cal," Cory said.

Now, on the television screen, outside The Rad, a woman reporter was seen interviewing some sort of senior police officer, with a lot of braid on his cap bill, but the sound was still the voice-over: "Captain Andrew Oldrum of State CID says there's reason to believe the other fugitive from the recent Massachusetts bank robbery was the driver of the getaway car."

Lindahl stared at Parker, who didn't look back, but shook his head. He needed Lindahl to remember not to act up in front of the Dennisons.

Now the interview was heard, or at least part of what Captain Oldrum had to say: "Given where they'd been spotted in the past, it looks as though they may be back-tracking now, which would be a smart move on their part, if they can get into an area we've already cleared."

"Captain Oldrum, why would they risk so much to commit what, in comparison, is a very small robbery, after the multi-hundred-thousand-dollar robbery in Massachusetts?"

"Well, Eve, we have reason to believe, from the one bandit we've apprehended so far, that they no longer have that money on them. Also, even if they still have some of it, the other two know from that first arrest their stolen money's too dangerous to spend, because we've got the serial numbers. So what they need is cash they can use without drawing attention to themselves. Still, this robbery seems like a pretty desperate move, so it looks like we're a lot closer to them than we thought earlier in the day."

Now the cut was to the television studio, where the same woman reporter smiled at the camera and said, "Police are asking anyone who might have been shopping at Willoughby Hills Center at the time of the robbery, and might have seen the fugitives, or their vehicle, or anything at all that seemed suspicious, to phone the special number on your screen—"

"Let's call it," Cal said. "We got him right here." Laughing at Lindahl, he said, "And you got to be the driver!"

"Shut up, Cal," Parker said. "Tom, switch off that set."

Cal, suddenly bristling, said, "My brother tells me to shut up. You don't tell me to shut up."

As Lindahl killed the sound on the television set, Parker took a step forward and slapped Cal hard, open-handed, across the cheek, under the patch. Cal jolted back, astonished and outraged. Parker stood watching him, hands at his sides, and Cal, fidgeting, wide eyed, tried to figure out something to do.

"Okay," Cory said, stepping forward, not quite between them, but just to the side, like a referee. "Okay, that's enough. If it goes any further, you got me, too."

Parker half turned to him. "They say it was definitely one of the guys they're looking for, and they say he was at this mall, and I'm not. But let's say your brother's right. They just said on the TV the bandits don't have the money any more, or if they do, they can't pass it because the law's got the serial numbers. So if I am the bandit, I either don't have the money or I have money nobody can use. And if I am the bandit, why weren't you two dead last night?"

Cory had nodded through all of that, thoughtful, and now he said, "I don't know."

"What do you know?"

"Something doesn't smell right." Cory nodded toward his brother but kept looking at Parker. "Cal and me, we both noticed it, and we talked about it."

Cal had apparently decided the slap on the face was now far enough in the past that he didn't have to react to it at all, so, his aggressive style back, he said, "What are you doin' here, that's the point. Whether you're him or you're not him, and I still know goddam well you're him, but even so, how come you're here? What are you doin here?"

"Visiting my old friend Tom."

"Bullshit," Cal said. "Maybe those old farts at the gun club bought it, but we don't. We never did. I took one look at you up at St. Stanislas and I said, 'What's goin on with that fella?' That was even before I looked at the picture."

Lindahl now stepped forward. He was paler than usual, and Parker could see he still hadn't completely adapted himself to what he'd just learned from the television set, but his expression was determined. "Cal," he said, "you never called me a liar before."

Cal turned to glower at him. "You gonna punch me now? I don't think so, Tom."

"Then don't call me a liar."

"Cal," Cory said, crowding in on top of whatever Cal had meant to say, "we're done in here."

Cal now had reason to glower at everybody. "Done in here? Whadaya mean done in here? Now the guy's knocking off shopping malls!"

"That's nothing to do with us," Cory told him. "Come on, Cal. Tom, I'm sorry we busted in on you."

"Anytime," Lindahl said, though he sounded angry. "Just knock first."

"We will. Come on, Cal. Sorry if we upset you, Ed."

"You didn't," Parker said.

"Well . . ." Cory herded Cal to the door and out, Cal wanting to yap on about something or other, Cory pushing him out with nods and hand gestures, the two finally outside, Cory closing the door without looking back.

Parker continued to stand and frown at the closed door. After a minute, Lindahl gave him a puzzled look. "What is it?"

Parker nodded at the door. "Cory's scheming," he said.

nine

Six hours. Six hours from now, Parker and Lindahl could leave Pooley and head south to the racetrack, which would be shut and dark and ready for them when they got there. That wasn't the problem; the problem was in the six hours.

Cory Dennison was out there somewhere, scheming, that was the first thing. He'd decided that, whoever Parker was, he was up to something the Dennison brothers would find interesting and should therefore be in on. So what would they do? Hang around the neighborhood? Watch Lindahl's house and SUV, follow them if they left? All the way to the racetrack?

All right; somewhere along the line he'd have to neutralize the brothers. But in a way, they were less trouble than Fred Thiemann, because they were at least sane and more or less sensible and knew what they wanted. Thiemann was none of those. He was a loose cannon, not at all under his own control, only partly under his wife's control. There was nothing Parker could do about him that wouldn't make it worse. If Thiemann were to die, at Parker's hands or his own or anybody else's, Parker would just have to forget the racetrack and hope to clear out of this part of the world before the law arrived.

Because once the law was interested in Thiemann, they would also be interested in Thiemann's partners in the manhunt. The wife would lead them to Lindahl, and that was the end.

What were the choices? He could tie up Lindahl right now, or shoot him if the man wanted to make trouble, and leave here in the SUV. He'd have the car's registration and the new driver's license belonging to William G. Dodd, and if stopped he'd say his friend Tom Lindahl had loaned him the car.

But if he did do that, and it turned out at the same time that Thiemann was eating his rifle, Parker would be on the road in a hot car and not know it. Or he could wait the six hours, ignoring the Dennison brothers and trusting Jane Thiemann to keep her husband in line, and the disaster would find him sitting here in Lindahl's living room with his feet up.

Another car. He needed a car he could safely drive, a car he could show up in at the roadblocks. A car with paperwork that wouldn't arouse suspicion, no matter what was happening back here in this neighborhood.

After the Dennisons left, Parker said, "I'll drive down to the corner, put some gas in the car."

Sounding bitter, Lindahl said, "Using some of the money you stole from that boy?"

Parker looked at him. "You got that wrong, Tom," he said. "I didn't take anything from that boy. I took some cash from a company has nine hundred stores. I needed the cash. You know that."

"You had that gun all along?"

"I'll be right back," Parker said, and turned to the door.

"No, wait."

Parker looked back and could see that Lindahl was trying to adjust his thinking. He waited, and Lindahl nodded and said, "All right. I know who you are, I already knew who you were. I shouldn't act as though it's any of my business."

"That's right."

"It's hard," Lindahl said. "It's hard to be around . . ."

The sentence trailed off, but Parker understood. It's hard to be around a carnivore. "It won't be for long," he said.

"No, I know. And I wanted to tell you," Lindahl hurried on, obviously in a rush to change the subject, "you don't want to go to that gas station on the corner. Go out to the right, eight miles, there's a Getty station. A straight run there and back."

"But this guy's right here. He's open on Sunday, I saw the sign."

"You don't want to go there," Lindahl insisted. "He

charges ten, fifteen cents more per gallon than anybody else."

"How does he get away with that?"

"He doesn't," Lindahl said. "The only people that stop there are tourists or lost."

"Then how does he make a living?"

"Social Security," Lindahl said. "And he sells lottery tickets there, that's mostly what people go to him for. A lot of people around here are nuts for the lottery. And he also does some repair work on cars."

"I saw some cars there, I didn't know if that meant he fixed them or sold them."

"He fixes them, he's a mechanic," Lindahl said. "That's what he mostly used to do, somewhere down in Pennsylvania. He worked for some big auto dealer down there. When he retired, he came up here and bought that station, because his wife's family came from around here somewhere."

"But why charge so much for gas?"

"Just crankiness," Lindahl said. "He's a loner, he likes working on engines and things, listening to the radio in his station."

"Is he a good mechanic?"

"Oh, yeah." Lindahl nodded, emphatic with it. "He'll do a good job on your car, and he won't cheat you, he's fair about that. That part he takes pride in. I've taken my own car to him, and he's been fine. What it is, he'll fix your car, but he doesn't want to talk to you. I think he likes cars more than people."

“What’s his name?”

“Brian Hopwood. But you don’t want to go there.”

“No, I’ll stay away from him,” Parker said. “I don’t need somebody cranky, that overcharges. The Getty station, you say, eight miles that way.”

“That’s what you want,” Lindahl agreed.

ten

The Dennisons' red Ram pickup was nowhere in sight as Parker drove a mile out of town, U-turned back past Lindahl's place tucked back in behind the boarded-up house, and stopped at the gas station, which was brightly lit in the daytime like most such places, but still had an air of emptiness about it.

There was one set of pumps, with service on both sides. Behind them was a broad low white clapboard building that was mostly overhead garage doors except for a small office at the right end with fuel additive posters obscuring the plate-glass window and the smaller panes of glass in the door. To the right of the building, along the rear line of the blacktop, were parked half a dozen older cars, all with license plates attached, so they were here for service, not for sale.

Parker got out of the Ford and read the hand-printed notice taped to each pump: PAY INSIDE FIRST. Taking out two of The Rad's twenties, he walked over to the office, where another hand-printed sign beside the door gave the hours of operation, including SUN 10–4.

He opened the door and heard the jangle of a warning bell, which was followed by classical music, something loud with a lot of strings that the bell had obscured for just an instant. Parker had expected a different kind of music, given Lindahl's description of Brian Hopwood, but that was the reason he'd come here, to understand the man and the operation.

The office was small and dark and crowded, as though brushed with a thin coating of oil. The desk was dark metal, covered with specs and repair books and appointment schedules and an old black telephone. A dark wood swivel chair behind it was very low, with the seat and back draped in a variety of cloth: old blankets, quilts, a couple of tan chamois cloths. On the back wall, a wooden shelf held an old cash register, next to a key rack with several sets of keys on it, each of them with a cardboard tag attached.

On the left wall of the office was an open doorway to the service area, through which a man now came, frowning as though he hadn't expected to be interrupted. He was short and scrawny and any age above Social Security eligibility. He wore what looked like army issue eyeglasses with the thin metal wings bent into dips and rises, and grease-covered work clothes. Wiping his hands on a small towel looped through his belt, he said, "Afternoon."

"Afternoon." Extending the twenties, Parker said, "I'm not sure it'll take that much. If not, I'll come back for change."

It was clear that Hopwood wasn't happy about that; two exchanges with a customer over one transaction. Still, he took the twenties, put them on the shelf in front of the cash register, and said, "Which pump you at?"

Parker peered through the poster-blocked window: "Three."

Hopwood bent behind the desk to set that pump and said, "I'll ring it up when you're done."

"Fine."

Hopwood was already on his way back to his work in the service area before Parker left the office. The man was without curiosity and would not be watching what Parker did, so he went first to the cars parked along the rear of the station blacktop. All were locked, their keys certainly on that rack in the office. A couple of them had personal items showing inside: a thermos, a blanket.

The law wanted people to keep their automobile registrations in their wallet or purse, but, in fact, most people leave it in the glove compartment with the insurance card, so at least some of these would be ready to go. If he needed one.

Parker went back to the Ford and pumped thirty-eight dollars and fifty cents' worth of gas. The car would have taken more than that, particularly with the high price Hopwood charged, but he wanted that second encounter.

Back in the office, Hopwood came from his work in response to the bell, and Parker said, "Sorry, that's all it took."

"Not a problem." Hopwood bent to see what the charge had come to.

"I'm staying with Tom Lindahl," Parker said.

"Thirty-eight-fifty. I recognized the car."

"On a little vacation."

"That right?" Hopwood made the transaction in the cash register and handed Parker a dollar bill and two quarters.

Parker said, "It says you close today at four."

"That's right." Squinting at the round white wall clock next to the service area entrance, Hopwood said, "You had plenty of time. An hour."

"When you close," Parker said, "is that it, you're closed, nobody here in case somebody shows up a little late? Or do you stay and work on the cars a little more?"

"Not me," Hopwood said, sounding almost outraged, as though somebody had asked him to lie under oath. "Four o'clock, I shut down, go home, say hello to the missus, have my shower, read the Sunday funnies until suppertime. I don't know what Tom Lindahl told you, but I'm not a nut."

"Tom said you were a good mechanic."

"Well, thank him for me." Nodding toward the Ford out by the pumps, he said, "I've managed to keep that thing going. Rides okay, doesn't it?"

"It does," Parker agreed. He pocketed his change, said, "Enjoy the funnies," and turned to leave.

eleven

"Just a minute," Hopwood said, and when Parker turned back, his hand not quite touching the doorknob, Hopwood had opened a drawer in his messy desk and now there was a tiny automatic pistol in his hand, its eye looking at Parker. Flat in the still-open drawer was a smudged copy of the artist's rendering.

"Maybe you'll put your hands on your head," Hopwood said.

Parker didn't. Instead, he gestured toward the picture in the drawer. "You don't think that's me, do you? This isn't even a joke any more."

"I'm not foolin, mister," Hopwood said. The automatic that almost disappeared inside his fist was small but serious, the Seecamp LWS32, with a magazine of six .32-caliber cartridges. With its one-inch barrel, it couldn't have much effect across a highway, but inside this room it would do the job.

Now Hopwood moved the gun-holding hand in a small arc, downward and to the right, to aim at Parker's left leg. "If I have to wing you, I will."

"I told you," Parker said, "I'm staying with Tom Lindahl. Call him if you want. That's his car right—"

"Last chance. Hands on top of your head."

With no choice, Parker started to lift his arms when the door directly behind him opened and somebody walked in. Hopwood lost his concentration as Parker took a quick step to his left, turning to see that the newcomer was the nosy woman who'd driven past him last night and stopped to ask him if she could help.

She was confused by the scene she'd walked into, reacting to the tension in the air but not yet noticing the small automatic closed in Hopwood's fist. "I'm sorry, did I—"

With both hands, Parker took her by the left elbow, spun, and threw her hard across the room and into Hopwood, who tried too late to backtrack out of the way, hitting the corner of his desk instead, knocking himself off balance. Then the woman crashed into him, and they fell diagonally in a jumble from the desk onto the floor. By the time they were separated and turned around and staring upward, Parker's pistol was in his hand.

"Stay right there," he said, and showed Hopwood the Ranger. "I don't wing."

"What is – what's—" She was still more bewildered than

anything else, but then she saw the Ranger in Parker's hand and her eyes widened and she cried, "You! You're the one stole Jack's gun!"

part three

one

Of the three men who'd pulled the bank job in Massachusetts, Nelson McWhitney was the only one who'd left the place carrying his own legitimate identification and driving his own properly registered pickup truck. The cops at the various roadblocks where he'd been stopped and the pickup searched had warned him against driving south toward the Mass Pike, because the heavy police activity had backed up traffic in all directions, so, even though his goal was Long Island, McWhitney drove steadily westward for hours, into the same areas where Parker found himself bogged down and Nick Dalesia found himself arrested.

He heard the news of the arrest on the truck radio and gave the radio an ironic nod and salute in response, saying, "Well, so long, Nick." A couple of miles farther on, having thought about it some more, he nodded and told the radio, "And so long money, too." That would be Nick's only bargaining chip, wouldn't it?

After Syracuse, McWhitney turned south, keeping to smaller roads because they were less backed up, but still making slow progress. He finally gave up and found a motel outside Binghamton, then early Sunday morning got up into a still-police-infested world and made his way southeast toward Long Island, where his home was and where the small bar he owned was and where he had an appointment coming up with a woman named Sharon.

On even a normal day, he would have known better than to drive through New York City to get to Long Island, and this was far from a normal day. It was amazing how much fuss three guys with a simple bank plan could create. And, of course, having grabbed Nick Dalesia, the law was now hungrier than ever to gobble up the other two.

Driving down across New York State, he found himself wondering, was he himself maybe a bargaining chip for Nick? He thought back, and he didn't believe he and Nick had shared that much private detail, not enough so that Nick could pinpoint McWhitney on Long Island. He hoped not.

What he'd do, when he finally got to the neighborhood, was case it first. If Nick did know enough about him to turn him up, the surveillance on his home and bar would be far too large for him not to notice. Just go there and see.

He stopped for lunch at a diner in Westchester, then headed south to the Throgs Neck Bridge to take him across to Long Island. The roadblock inspection at the bridge was the most thorough and intense yet, but then, once he got on the Island, life suddenly became much calmer. There were only a limited number of routes on and off the Island, so clearly the authorities believed they hadn't so far let any of the bank robbers through.

His neighborhood was quiet, like any Sunday afternoon. His bar, where he'd left a guy he knew in charge while he took his little "vacation," was also very quiet, almost empty-looking, which was also standard for a Sunday afternoon.

McWhitney parked the truck in the alley behind his building, went into his empty and stuffy-smelling apartment, opened a few windows, opened a beer, and switched on CNN. No further news on the bank-robbing front.

He wondered how Parker was doing among the straights.

two

Brian Hopwood, asprawl on his back on his dirty office floor, grinding pain in his left side where his rib cage had smacked into the sharp corner of his desk, useless little toy automatic still clutched in his fist, stared up past Suzanne Gilbert's thick mass of wavy auburn hair at the hardcase he'd been stupid enough to try to get the drop on, and he thought, Well, I'm not dead, so that's good.

Yes, it was good. If this hardcase here, this bank robber, had just wanted to clear these two pests out of his path, he'd have shot them without a word, without a warning like, "I don't wing." So in fact, he didn't want to shoot them, not unless they made it necessary.

Brian Hopwood had lived this long a time partly by never making it necessary for anybody to shoot him, and he was prepared to go on that way the rest of his life. Which meant shutting up Suzanne here. Heavier than she looked, now draped across him like a deer carcass lashed to a fender, half-twisted around with her elbow propping her torso up by bearing down into Hopwood's stomach, she glared in discovery and outrage at the hardcase who had their lives in his hands, yelling at him, "You! You're the one stole Jack's gun!" As though this were Twenty questions or something.

Jack Riley? It would have to be Jack Riley, but what the hell would Jack Riley want with a gun? Fighting that off, fighting his mind's habit of digression – that's what made him the first-rate loner mechanic he was, in a job that let his mind wander wherever it would while his hands and some other parts of his brain dealt with the particular problems of this particular automobile of the moment – Brian yelled, or tried to yell in a raspy hoarse croak that was all he seemed to have right now, "Suzanne, shut up and get off me! Mister, I'm putting the gun down, see? On the floor here, I can give it a push if you— Suzanne, get off me!"

She managed it, finally, rolling rightward off him, rolling over completely in a flurry of legs and tossing hair. She was dressed in black slacks and a gray wool sweater, so she didn't flash any parts of herself, but Brian's digression-ready brain did notice there was something very nicely womanly about that body in motion.

The hardcase hadn't moved, but now he pointed a finger of his left hand at Suzanne while holding the revolver still trained on Brian, and said to Suzanne, "Right there's good."

Suzanne had wound up in a splay-legged seated position,

and did move some more, folding her legs in close into something like a loose lotus position while she glared up at him, but at least she didn't say anything else.

Then, as though Suzanne had been by that order effectively locked into a cage and put out of play, the hardcase looked at Brian again and said, "Tell me about her."

Tell me about her? She's right here; why doesn't he ask her himself?

He's the man with the gun, Brian, he gets to do it any way he wants. Brian said, "Her name's Suzanne Gilbert. She works nights at Holy Mary Hospital in emergency room admittance. Her grandfather lives just down that way."

"Jack?"

"Jack Riley, yeah, that's her grandfather."

And now Suzanne spoke up again; doesn't she understand the situation here? Apparently not, because, sounding aggrieved, she said, "Why did you take Jack's gun?"

He looked at her, and though his face didn't change into anything you could call a smile, Brian still had the feeling the question had given him some kind of amusement. "Just in case Brian here," he told her, "would draw down on me. You didn't stop to see your grandfather last night."

Last night? Brian looked from the hardcase to Suzanne, who didn't even look worried, much less scared, and he thought, What about last night? Now there was some other story here, and he wasn't in on it.

She said, "No, I just drive by, on my way home.

Sometimes he can't sleep, and, if that happens, he'll sit out on his porch with the light on and I stop and we talk awhile. He knows I'll be there and it makes it easier for him, so these days he's sleeping more than he used to. Last night when I went by he was asleep in front of the television set, so that was fine, so I just went on home. I suppose that's when you broke in and stole his gun."

For Christ's sake, Suzanne, Brian thought, leave it alone. But the hardcase didn't mind. He just shrugged and said, "He didn't seem to use it much." Then he switched those cold eyes to Brian, considered him a minute as though he might decide after all he was the kind of pest you might as well shoot, and said, "When did you decide?"

"To be a hero?" Brian, beyond embarrassment, shrugged and looked away. "When I did it."

The truth was, it had grown in him. The customer had come in the door, had given him two twenties and said he was at pump number three, and went out again. Brian had gone back to the brake drum repair he meant to finish before four o'clock closing time, and as he'd worked, his wandering mind gradually put together that customer's face with one of the two Wanted posters he'd put in his desk drawer because he hadn't wanted to throw away something given to him by the troopers but on the other hand didn't want to put those two faces on the wall to be an irritation and a distraction all the time. In very short order, the two faces had blended into one and he'd known the customer out there pumping gas was one of the bank robbers everybody was looking for. Driving Tom Lindahl's car, so God knows what had happened to Tom.

What to do about the bank robber? He'd decided it was a toss of the dice. If the guy pumped his forty bucks' worth and drove away, then the next time Brian stepped into the office he'd call the state troopers and tell them he believed he'd just seen one of the bank robbers in Tom Lindahl's car, and leave it up to them to catch the fellow. But if he came back in for change, that would be a message to Brian from On High that it was up to him to do the citizen's arrest thing himself. He had his little automatic in the drawer, and the sequence seemed simple: pull out the gun, hold the robber, call the troopers, wait.

Well, that sure worked out well, didn't it?

The hardcase must have been thinking the same thing, because he next said, "You'd have done better to wait till I was gone, then call the law."

"Oh, I know that," Brian said. "If you'd used up the forty and didn't come back in, that's what I was gonna do."

"Well, then, Brian," the hardcase said, "that should use up your stupidity for today, shouldn't it?"

"I sure hope so."

"So if I tell you to call your wife and say you're gonna be late, don't hold supper, might be nine or ten o'clock, you aren't going to be cute, are you?"

"Well, I never do that," Brian said. As long as he was

relatively safe, he wanted to go on being relatively safe. "If I say that to her," he explained, "she'll know something's wrong, I won't have to try anything cute."

The hardcase waved that away, shaking his head and the pistol, focusing Brian's attention. "You got an important customer," he said, "or a close friend, somebody's got an emergency, got to drive to a wedding somewhere tomorrow, you've really got to get his car done."

Surprisingly, Suzanne spoke up at that. "Dr. Hertzberg," she said.

The hardcase looked at her. "Who's that?"

She said, "He treats a lot of the people around here. My grandfather." She looked at Brian. "And you."

"I suppose," Brian said. And he realized she was right, it was plausible.

The hardcase studied him, thinking about it. "If your wife doesn't buy it," he said, "I can't leave you two here."

"I know that," Brian told him. "Suzanne's right, Dr. Hertzberg's the one man I'd stay here for, work late. All right, I'll call her."

"Good. Suzanne, you stay where you are. Brian, get up and sit at the desk, and make every move slow and out in the open."

"Oh, I will," Brian promised, and did. His ribs gave him a few nasty jolts as he struggled upward, using the same corner of the desk for support that had earlier punched him, and when he was at last on his feet, he was breathing hard, as though he'd been running. The hard breaths were also painful, so he turned slowly and eased himself down into his desk chair, and then the pain receded and the breathing got easier.

"Give me a minute to catch my breath," he said, "think out what I want to say."

"Go ahead."

Brian looked over at Suzanne, and she was frowning at him with some sort of question in her eyes, but he couldn't figure out what. He'd known her for years, a pleasant if somewhat bossy woman, a granddaughter of a neighbor, but he didn't actually know her very well. He wasn't the sort to chat up a divorced woman, living on her own the last few years, so when she frowned at him like that, her eyes full of some sort of puzzlement, he had no idea what she might be thinking, what it was she wanted to know.

"Do it now."

"Oh," Brian said, and looked at the phone. "Right."

Picking up the receiver, he noticed for the first time that some of the phone's buttons were much dirtier than the others. His hands were always dirty when he was working here, so, of course, those buttons must be dirtier because the number he most often called was his own home, to speak to Edna.

Yes; he tapped out the sequence on the dirtier buttons, and on the second ring Edna answered: "Three seven five two."

"Edna, it's me. I gotta stay and work late tonight."

"Wha'd, you find a tootsie?"

"Sure. We're going to Miami Beach together."

"Without your supper? That'll be the day."

"Well, that's the thing. Dr. Hertzberg, you know, he's gotta go to a wedding tomorrow down in Pennsylvania, he's got some real coolant problems here in that clunker he drives, I promised I'd have it for him first thing in the morning."

"I'm doing chicken curry."

"It'll reheat."

"Men. How late are you gonna be?"

"Maybe nine, ten."

"Why not just trade him a new car?"

"Listen, I'm not gonna argue with Dr. Hertzberg. He wants to go to that wedding."

She sighed, long and sincere. "And the man's a saint, I know, I know. I'm not gonna reheat it with you, I'm gonna eat it when it's ready and tastes like something."

He knew she wouldn't, she'd wait for him, and he found himself hoping very hard she wasn't going to have to wait forever. Just keep going along with the guy, just be grateful the guy was professional enough he didn't start blasting away the first time he saw an amateur with a gun, and a little later on tonight that chicken curry, reheated or not reheated, would be the most tasty thing he ever ate in his entire life.

"Well," he said, "I'll get there just as soon as I can."

"Say hello to the good doctor for me."

"Oh, yeah, I will."

It wasn't till he hung up that his hands started to tremble, but then they did a real dance. He was inside this sudden airless bowl here, and he'd made contact with the normal world outside the bowl, and it had shaken him much more than he'd guessed.

The hardcase, standing over by the door, said, "That's good, you did that fine."

"Thanks."

"Now I want the laces out of those boots."

"Sure," Brian said, knowing what that meant. It meant, unless something brand-new went wrong, he was going to live through this.

What he wore at the garage, because he was surrounded there by large, heavy, dirty things in motion, some of them also sharp, was steel-cap-reinforced boots, laced up past the ankle. He bent now to strip the laces out of the boots, and the hardcase said, "You got a Closed sign?"

"Over there, tucked in behind that file cabinet."

He went on stripping out the laces, and then the hardcase said, "You use this sign?"

"Every night."

"It says 'Closed' on one side, 'Open' on the other. How come you don't use the Open side?"

"People know if I'm here." The truth was, and Brian knew

it, he didn't use the Open side because he thought it sounded like an invitation for a whole lot of people to come in and chat and fill up his day; who needed it?

The hardcase said, "Where do you put it? Window or door?"

"It goes in the bottom right corner of the window. It slips in a space between the glass and the wood there. Here's the laces."

"Put them on the desk. Suzanne, get up. Slow! Come over here, pick up one of those laces. Brian, put your hands behind your back. Suzanne, tie his wrists together and then tie them to the metal crossbar on the chair. Go ahead."

"I don't know why you're doing—"

"Now."

Brian felt the rough movements of the shoelace wrapping around his crossed wrists as the hardcase said, "Not so tight the blood stops, but not loose. I'll check it when you're done."

"I was a Girl Scout," she said. "I know knots."

It felt to him she was doing it pretty tight. Had he read in a book somewhere where people could defeat being tied up by tensing certain muscles here and there? Well, maybe somebody could.

"All right, Suzanne, stand straight, wrists crossed behind you."

"I don't want somebody to tie me up."

"I tie you up, or I kill you. Kill you might be easier for

both of us, you won't be tense any more. I only do it this way because it gives the cops less motivation."

The silence seemed to Brian to go on too long. If the guy shot Suzanne, wouldn't he have to shoot Brian, too? The cops would already be motivated, anyway.

Suzanne, wake up! Don't you know what we've got here?

But then the silence changed in quality, and it seemed to Brian he could hear the little sounds of the laces moving against flesh. No more discussion followed, no more argument; all to the good.

"All right, Suzanne, you're gonna sit against the wall here, I'll help you down. Fine. Legs out straight."

Brian's chair was on small casters that didn't work very well, but he could push himself back from the desk and turn just enough to see Suzanne seated on the floor, back straight, against the side wall, and the hardcase now down on one knee in front of her, tying her ankles with a brand-new set of jumper cables. Finishing, he looked over at Brian and said, "That chair rolls. I don't like that."

"I'm sorry," Brian said.

The hardcase got to his feet and went into the shop, where they heard him rummaging around. When he came back, he had some tools in his hands and a long roll of black electric tape. Putting it all on the desk, not saying anything else now, he moved Brian, chair and all, into the front right corner of the room, next to the door, with Suzanne on the floor to his other side. From here, of course, nobody out by the pumps looking in here would be able to see either of them.

The hardcase checked Brian's wrists and must have been satisfied, because then he used the electric tape to tie Brian's white-socked ankles to the chair legs, and used screwdrivers as chocks to keep the casters from moving. Finally he fastened the screwdrivers to the floor and the casters with more electric tape.

He was done with talking, apparently, and barely looked at them any more as he went about his work. Finished, he stepped back to look at what he'd done, while they both mutely watched. Then he went over to the key rack on the back wall, considered the keys and the identifying cards, and chose one. From where he sat, Brian thought he'd picked Jeff Eggleston's Infiniti, the best car he had here right now.

That was all. The hardcase came over to open the door, figure out the push-button lock arrangement, and, without giving them a glance, he left. From his position, Brian couldn't tell if he drove off in the Infiniti or Tom Lindahl's SUV.

"The arrogance of that man!" Suzanne cried. "To do a thing like this to perfect strangers, no excuse, no reason, no— I've never seen such a horrible, horrible . . ." She couldn't seem to figure out how to end the sentence.

"Suzanne," Brian said, trying to be kindly, to calm her down, "who he is, the situation he's in, he's gonna do pretty much what he wants."

Now Suzanne turned her outrage on Brian, as though it were all his fault (which it almost was). Voice dripping with scorn, caustically she demanded, “Oh, yes? Why? Is he supposed to be somebody famous?”

Brian stared at her. He thought, It’s gonna be a long night.

three

Cal glowered out his side of the windshield as Cory drove the pickup truck. "If he was the guy, we'd be dead now," he quoted, twisting the words as though he wanted to spit. "That guy talks pretty big, Cory. We should of called his bluff right there."

"That doesn't do us any good."

"Does me some good." Cal looked around, and they were out in the country, Pooley well behind them. "Where we goin?"

"To Judy's."

Their sister, younger than them, living on her own since the guy she thought she was going to marry went into the navy instead. "What for?"

"To borrow her car."

Cal scoffed. "Judy won't give us her car."

Watching the road, Cory said, "She won't give it to you. She'll loan it to me."

"Why? What do we want with her little dinky car?"

"We have to have a different vehicle," Cory told him, "because Tom and that other guy know this truck. They'll see it in their rearview mirror, they'll know just what we're up to."

"Oh. Yeah, sure, naturally," Cal said, trying to pretend he'd thought of it himself, or at least might have. Then, needing to prove he could think of the details, too, he said, "But how you gonna get her to give it to you? You show up in this, you already got wheels, then you say, 'Gimme your car,' what are you gonna say? Because we're gonna take down a bank robber?"

"I got a job interview," Cory said.

Cal gave him a skeptical look. "What job interview?"

"I say I got a job interview. At that community college, in the computer arts department."

"They already turned you down over there."

"I know they did, and so does Judy." Cory nodded at the road ahead, agreeing with himself. "So what I tell Judy, I got another interview over there, this time I'm not gonna dress like a farmer and I'm not gonna show up in some pickup truck. I'm gonna dress like a guy teaches computer arts, and I'm gonna show up in Judy's nice Volkswagen Jetta. I'll tell her, and it's true, I'll even run it through the car wash first."

"Judy's down on me, you know," Cal pointed out. "If she sees me, she's gonna say, 'What are you taking that bozo to college for?'"

Cory laughed. “You’re right,” he said. “I can’t have you in the truck when I get there. It’s got to be just Judy and me.”

“So whadaya gonna do with me while you’re off bullshitting Judy?”

“There’s that diner about a mile before her place,” Cory reminded him.

“Randall’s.”

“That’s the one. I’ll let you off, you have a cup of coffee—”

“Or a beer.”

“Make it a cup of coffee. We gotta be sharp tonight, Cal.”

“Okay, okay, I’ll make it coffee. And you go off to Judy by yourself.”

“And come back with the Jetta.”

“And that so-called tough guy won’t have an idea in the world we’re sitting right on his ass.”

“Right.”

Cal frowned at the windshield, struck by a sudden thought. “What if they’re already gone when we get back?”

“Whatever they’re gonna do,” Cory assured him, “they won’t start in on it until after dark.”

And that also made sense. Cal nodded at the road awhile, thinking, then said, “What do you suppose they’re up to?”

“We’ll find out when we see them do it,” Cory said, and that was the end of that conversation until they reached the diner, a sprawling place that had originally been a little railroad car type of greasy spoon, but then kept adding on dining rooms and kitchens and bigger neon signs out front until now it looked more like an Indian casino than a place to eat. It was at the intersection of the smallish state road they were on and a bigger U.S. highway, and was always pretty full, though the food wouldn't bring anyone back.

Cory stopped near the entrance and said, "I'll be maybe half an hour."

"I'll sit by the window," Cal told him as he opened his door.

"Just have coffee, Cal, okay?"

"Sure, sure. Don't worry about me."

Cal got out, Cory drove away, and Cal went into the diner, where he had a cheeseburger, onion rings, and a beer.

four

Usually Fred spent Sunday afternoons in fall and winter watching football games by himself in the living room while Jane read in the enclosed back porch that was a greenhouse in summer and the best view of the outside world in winter. Today, though, when she got home from Tom Lindahl's place with the rifle, though Fred was in the living room as usual, the television set was off and he was just sitting there, in his regular chair, slumped, not even looking toward the set but downward, past his knees at the carpet on the floor, brooding. He barely lifted his head when she walked in, trying to be chipper, saying, "I never knew this thing was so heavy."

"Oh, you got it," he said, though without much animation. "Good."

"Should I put it in the closet?"

"Sure. Okay."

She started out of the room, but couldn't help herself, had to turn back and say, "No football?"

"Ah, it's just same-old, same-old," he said, and shrugged, and didn't exactly meet her eye.

She herself had always thought football games were very much same-old, same-old, the same movements seen every Sunday, like ritual Japanese theater, only the costumes changing, but she didn't like to hear that sentiment come from Fred. She only nodded, though, and went to the bedroom and put the rifle in its place at the back of the closet, upright, leaning against the left rear corner. Then she went back to the living room, where Fred had not moved, and said, "I saw that man."

He roused a bit. "Uh? Oh, him."

"He's very strange, Fred."

"He knows what he wants," Fred said, which seemed to her a strange kind of remark.

"He did say something," she went on, "that I thought was odd, but maybe it was a good thing to say."

No response. She waited for him to ask what the strange man had said, but he didn't even look at her, so she had to go ahead without prompting. "He said George will want to see you when he gets home."

"George?" Not as though he didn't remember their own son, but as though he couldn't imagine why they'd been discussing him.

"Tom told him," she explained. "And he said George would want to see you when he gets home."

"Of course, he's going to see me," Fred said, starting to get irritated. "What do you mean?"

"Well – just that we'll be together again."

He frowned, trying to understand, then suddenly looked angry and said, "Because I wanted my rifle back? It's my rifle."

"I know that, Fred."

"It's in the closet. You asked me, and I said put it in the closet. What do you people think of me?"

"I told you, it was just this odd thing he said, that's all."

"He'd like that, wouldn't he?" Fred said, looking sullen now. "Solve all of his problems for him, wouldn't it?"

"What problems, Fred? Now I don't know what you're talking about."

"Nothing," he said, turning farther away, brushing the air with his hands. "It isn't anything. Thank you for bringing it back."

Which was clearly a dismissal, so she went away again, paused at the kitchen to make herself a cup of instant coffee, and then went onto the porch, where the book she was currently reading waited for her on the seat of her chair.

Jane loved to read. Reading invariably took her out of the world she lived in, out of this glassed-in porch with its changing views of the seasons, and off to some other world with other views, other people, other seasons. Invariably; but not today.

Jane tended to buy best sellers, but only after they came out in paperback, so the excited buzz that had greeted the book's initial appearance had cooled and she could see the story for itself, with its insights and its failings. She was a forgiving reader, even when she was offered sequences that didn't entirely make sense; after all, now and again the sequence of actual life didn't make sense, either, did it?

Like that man Smith, staying with Tom Lindahl. What could possibly have brought those two together? And how had Tom, a man she'd known for probably thirty years, suddenly come up with an "old friend" nobody'd ever heard of before?

No; that was the real world. What she was trying to concentrate on was the world inside this book, and finally, after distracting herself several times, she did succeed, and settled in with these characters and their story. Now she concentrated on the problems of these other relationships and intertwining histories and didn't look up until the room had grown so dark she simply couldn't read any more.

Turning to switch on the floor lamp to her left, she glanced at her watch and saw it was well after seven. Oh, and they hadn't done anything about supper.

Usually, by now, Fred would have come back to tell her the game was over, and sit with her to decide about Sunday supper, which was a much looser arrangement now that Jodie had gone off to Penn State. But today there was no football, no end of game, and no Fred.

Was he going to just sit in there in the living room

forever and brood? It had to be much darker in there than out here on the porch, but when she looked toward the doorway, she could see no light at all from inside the house.

Was there something frightening in there, in the dark? Was there something unfamiliar in there, like an unread book, but not one she would enjoy? There was something frightening somewhere, she was sure of that, something she didn't like at all, like a horror movie at the moment when you know something bad is about to happen.

But that was nothing at all, that was just nerves. That was her house in there.

Had he fallen asleep? That might even be a blessing, and even more so if he woke feeling better about things. But she should make sure, so she put the bookmark in the book, got to her feet, and moved through the house, switching the lights on along the way.

The living room was empty. She looked toward the bedroom and called, "Fred?" No answer.

Suddenly really frightened, in a more horrible way than any book or horror movie had ever frightened her, she went to the front door to look out. Their garage was full of junk, so the Taurus was always parked in the driveway. It was very dark out there now, and the Taurus was black, so she had to switch on the outside light to be sure the Taurus was not there.

Where was he? What had he done? More and more afraid, almost not wanting the answers to the questions that crowded her mind, she hurried to the bedroom and opened the closet door.

The rifle was gone.

five

"It's night," Tom said, and looked from the window back at the guy he'd grown used to thinking of as Ed, even though he knew that could not possibly in any way be his name. "When do you want to go?"

Ed rose and came over to glance outside. "A little change of plan," he said.

Tom didn't like the sound of that. It was very hard to keep up with what was going on here, with the Pandora's box he'd opened when he'd first seen Ed pulling himself up that hill ahead of the dogs, and when he'd decided to use the man instead of turning him in. That snap decision, born out of frustration and self-contempt, had consequences that just kept echoing, so that Tom almost had the feeling that, without intending to do so, he'd become a rodeo rider, a fellow on a bucking bronco for the first time in his life, where it would be a disaster beyond belief if he were to fall off.

Wondering if his voice was shaking, he said, "Isn't it late for a new plan? You don't want to do it tonight, after all?"

"No, it's tonight. The change is, you drive down by yourself."

"By myself?" Alarmed, Tom said, "I thought we were doing this together."

"We are. When you get there, that first place you unlocked, you wait. If I'm not there, I'll show up a little later."

"But—" Tom tried to understand what was happening. Ed didn't have a car. He didn't have anybody else here he could ask for help. How was he going to get all the way from here to the track?

"How are you going to get there?"

"I'll get there," Ed said. "You don't have to know what I'm doing."

"I don't get this," Tom said. He didn't just feel confused, he felt very nervous, as though he were at the edge of a cliff or something. A nauseous kind of fear was rising in him, giving him that rotten taste of bile in the back of his throat. "I don't see why you have to change things."

"You'll see when it's over. Listen, Tom."

Reluctantly, Tom said, "I'm listening."

"You leave here, you drive down there. If you see Cory's truck anytime, don't worry about it."

"Why? Are you going to be driving it?"

"No, just don't worry about it. Keep driving. When you get there, wait. If I don't show up in half an hour, you can go do the thing yourself, or you can just turn around and come back, up to you. But I will show up."

"You've got something else going on."

Ed gave him an exasperated look. "We work from different rule books, Tom. You already know that."

"Yes."

Why did I think I could control him? Tom thought, remembering the sight of the man coming up that hill. Because he was on the run? That didn't make him somebody that could be controlled, that made him somebody that could never be controlled.

Ed said, "This'd be a good time for you to go."

Startled, Tom thought, I'm still supposed to go! I'm still supposed to do this. For Christ's sake, Tom, you're not the assistant on this thing, it's your theft. You're the one thought of it, you're the one wanted to hurt those bastards at Gro-More with it, and you're the one brought this man into it. And it's still yours.

Very nervous, but knowing there was no choice, Tom looked around his little living room and said, "You'll turn the lights off?"

"Go, Tom."

"All right." Tom looked over at the parrot and saw the parrot was looking directly back at him. Why didn't I ever name it? he wondered. I'll do it now. When I get back. No, while I'm driving down there, I'll think of a name.

six

When it started to turn to night, Jack Riley switched the porch light on. That always brought Suzanne, but tonight it didn't. Where was she?

Four hours. More than four hours ago, she was right here, they were talking about who around here would sneak into a man's house and steal his gun, and she said she'd go off and get some gas and something for them to have supper together, and off she drove.

Jack figured, maybe an hour. He didn't happen to look to see which way she went when she drove off, so she might have gone to Brian Hopwood's gas station here in town, or she might have gone out to the Getty station, the other way, all depending on where she figured to pick up something for their supper. So maybe half an hour, maybe an hour; no more.

A little after six, he woke up in front of the television set – again! . . . and cursed himself for it. He kept promising himself and promising himself, no more sleeping in front of the television set. He'd tell himself what to do: At the first feeling of sleepiness, get up, stand up, walk around. Go outside, maybe. If the lights weren't on, turn them on. Just do anything instead of falling asleep yet again in front of the goddam TV.

Well, he couldn't do it. He'd be sitting there, watching some damn thing, wide awake, and the next he'd know, it would be two or three or four hours later, and he was waking up in front of the set again, mouth dry, head achy, bones stiff.

Damn, how could he stop that? Stand up, maybe? Never watch television sitting down, only stand up in front of the set? Or would he fall asleep standing up and break his nose when he hit the floor?

Women are supposed to outlive you, dammit. They're supposed to be there to give you a poke in the ribs when they see you nodding off. Just another way life was a pain in the butt without Eileen.

Jack Riley was nine years a widower. He'd lived the last seven years in this house, once he'd understood his former home was too much for him to care for on his own, and the money the house had sold for was better off in blue-chip stocks. In the years since his moving here, Suzanne was just about his closest female companion, very different from Eileen, and one of the differences was that it was no way her job description to sit next to him all the time and poke him in the ribs when he started to fall asleep in front of the goddam television set.

Where was Suzanne? How far could she have gone in search of gas and food? There hadn't been an accident, had there?

If only he'd been looking out the window when she drove off, so now he'd have some sort of idea where she might be. At Brian Hopwood's station? It was after six, and he knew Brian was long closed by now, but he tried calling the gas station number, anyway, just in case, and, of course, it rang and rang and rang over there in that empty building, where Brian Hopwood would be the last man in the world to install an answering machine.

The other way, maybe? Jack didn't know anybody at the Getty station, and in any case she would have been through there long ago. Back here long ago, if everything was all right.

Jack switched the television off before he sat down again because he didn't want to fall asleep, dammit, he wanted to be wide-awake for when she got home, and in the meantime he wanted to be wide-awake so he could fret.

It had all begun last night, when, having awakened in front of the television set yet again, he'd finally got himself out of his living room chair and into bed. He'd become a creature of many habits since he'd been in this house on his own, and one of those habits, the last thing every night, just as he was getting into bed, was to unlock the drawer in the bedside table and look in at the pistol sitting there.

It was reassuring, when you lived alone in an isolated place like this, to know that little protective device was there. He'd never actually fired the gun; he'd only bought it for the sense of security it gave him, but that sense of security was real – it helped him to sleep soundly every night – and so the ritual was there, at bedtime, to look in for just a second at the gun. Like a pet you're saying good night to.

And last night it was gone. That was a real stomach-churner of a moment. He'd been half-seated on the bed, opening the drawer, and he bolted right up again when he saw that empty space where the gun was supposed to be. Then he stared around wildly, looking for an explanation, trying to remember a moment in which he himself would have moved the gun to some other location – where? – and found no such moment, nor any reason for any such moment.

The next thing he'd done was go through the whole house again, making sure every door and window was shut and locked, and they all were. So had it been sometime during the day that the gun was taken? But who would know he had it, or where to find it, or where to find the key?

He knew the few people who lived in this town, and there wasn't a one of them he could even begin to imagine sneaking into this house and making off with his gun. But who else? Some passing bum? There were no passing bums, no foot traffic at all. Somebody driving by in a car wouldn't suddenly stop and walk into Jack Riley's house and walk out with his gun. It made no sense, no matter how you looked at it.

Feeling totally spooked, he then switched on the front porch light, as though it might attract Suzanne at this late hour, but almost immediately switched it off again, because he knew it wouldn't attract Suzanne in the middle of the night and he didn't want to know who else it might attract. Instead, he left lights on in the bathroom and the kitchen, and thus did get some sleep, though not as much as usual, and this morning he called Suzanne to tell her about it.

She was as baffled as he was, of course. She had other things she had to do on Sunday morning, but could come over to see him this afternoon, and did. When she arrived, again he told the story. She double-checked all his doors and windows, helped him look in all the other drawers in the house, then sat down to try to figure out who might have done it.

No suspects came to mind. Eventually Suzanne said she'd go off for gas and supper, and Jack fell asleep in front of the goddam television again, and now what?

Suzanne gone four hours. Night outside. No gun, no Suzanne. Sometime after seven, he accepted the fact that there was no alternative; he had to call the troopers.

He didn't want to. If it turned out there was some simple rational explanation for the disappearance – both disappearances – he'd feel like a fool, some old geezer that's lost his marbles. But the gun is really gone, and Suzanne really hasn't come back, so eventually there was just nothing else to do.

Jack kept all the emergency numbers written on a piece of cardboard tacked to the wall near the kitchen phone, including the nearby state police barracks, because they were the ones responsible for policing this area. Still reluctant, but knowing he just had to do it, he dialed the number, and after a minute a voice came on and said, "Barracks K, Trooper London."

"Hello," Jack said. "I wanna report – well, I wanna report two things."

"Yes, sir. Your name, sir?"

"First I— Oh. Riley. John Edward Riley."

"Your address, sir?"

"Route 34, Pooley," he said, and gave the house number, and then the trooper wanted to know his phone number, and only then did he show any interest in the reason for the call. "You say you want to make a report?"

"A disappearance," Jack said. "Two disappearances."

"Family members, sir?"

"Well, it's— No, wait. The first was last night, was the gun."

"The gun, sir?"

"I've got – I had— When I moved here, I bought this little pistol, it's called a Ranger, I got the permit and all, you know, it's for house defense."

"Yes, sir. And it disappeared?"

"Last night. I keep it locked in a drawer, and last night, before I went to bed, I went to look at it, be sure everything was okay, and it wasn't there."

"Sir, did you have any reason to believe everything was not okay?"

"Not till I saw the gun wasn't there."

"Sir, did you have a reason to look for the gun?"

"I always do. Every night, I just double-check."

"Yes, sir, I see. Could you tell me who else resides with you, sir?"

"Just me, I'm on my own."

"Did you have guests, visitors, yesterday, sir?"

"No, it was just me. You see, that's why it doesn't make any sense."

"Did you report the disappearance, sir?"

"Just now. I mean no, not till now. This morning I called my granddaughter, Suzanne, she came over this afternoon, we looked for it, but it's gone. Then, around three o'clock, she went out, she had to get gas and she was gonna get something for our supper, and she never came back."

"This is your granddaughter, sir?"

"Suzanne. Suzanne Gilbert."

So then he had to tell the trooper everything about Suzanne, her looks and her age and her weight and her employment and a whole lot of stuff that didn't seem to Jack as though it mattered, but he figured, it's the trooper's job, let him do it. And after that, there was a lot about

Suzanne's car. And after that, he wanted to know everything about Suzanne's personal life; was she married, did she have a boyfriend, was anybody living with her, had she ever gone off on her own before? And through it all, Jack couldn't figure out, from the even, flat way the trooper asked his questions, whether he was being taken seriously or patronized. Because, if there was one hint that he was being patronized, boy, would he start to holler. Never mind the gun; we're talking about Suzanne here!

But then at last the trooper said, "We'll dispatch a car, sir. They should be there in less than half an hour."

By God, Jack thought, I hope Suzanne's back by then, and yet, on the other hand, I hope she isn't. Nothing bad happen to her, just not already here when the troopers show up.

"Thank you," he said. "I'll leave the porch light on."

seven

It wasn't football Fred saw on the blank television screen, it was the cell. The all-purpose cell, sometimes the one he knew he was headed for, sometimes the one George was in right now – what has happened to our family? – but other times the cell/grave in which lay the man he killed, twitching still in death.

He had never seen George's cell, of course, so this cell, constantly shifting, existed only in his imagination, fed mostly by old black-and-white movies watched on nights he couldn't sleep. A small stone room it was, longer than wide, high-ceilinged, with hard iron bars making up one of the short walls and one small high-up window in the opposite wall, showing nothing but gray. The cell smelled of damp and decay. He lay curled on the floor there, or George did, or sometimes that poor man up at Wolf Peak, the last thick dark red blood pulsing out of his back.

It was getting dark outside the living room windows.

Imagination had never much bothered Fred before this, but now he was all imagination, screaming nerve ends of imagination, imagining the cell, imagining the shame, and now, as darkness was coming on, imagining the teeth. Destroying the evidence. It gets darker and darker, and all those rustling creatures gather around the body on the forest floor, gnawing at it, snarling at one another, gnawing and gnawing.

His body. The way he sometimes became George, in that Gothic prison cell, now sometimes, too, he became the dead man on Wolf Peak, among all those jaws, all those teeth.

I can't stand this, he thought, I have to get out of this, and what he meant was, he could no longer stand his mind, he had to get away from his mind, and, of course, he understood what he meant by that.

But what stopped him? Not thoughts of his family, his wife, his son, his daughter, they'd get over him after a while, everybody gets over everybody sooner or later. Not cowardice; he had no fear of eating the rifle, he knew the terror would be short and the pain almost nonexistent.

What stopped him was the thought of that man Smith. Ed Smith, or whoever he was. To send that message home with Jane, to play his little psychological games again, the way he'd done up in the woods, the way he'd done on the drive home. Manipulating him. Sending Jane home with a coded message – don't kill yourself – because the real code under the first code was to put the idea of killing himself into his head.

That's what Smith had in mind, that was so obvious. Pretend sympathy – as though that man knew the meaning of the word "sympathy" – as a way to put that little worm into his brain: Wouldn't it be easier if you were dead?

God, yes, it would. God, he didn't need Ed Smith to tell him that. But with Smith everywhere around him, it was just impossible. No matter how much pain he was in, no matter how hopeless everything was, he couldn't kill himself, he just couldn't, for the one and only reason that he wouldn't give a bastard like Ed Smith the satisfaction.

Time went on, and his thinking circled around the same points, but gradually the angles shifted, gradually he came around to another point of view. If only Ed Smith were gone. It would be possible to become unstuck, to move forward with life, if only Ed Smith were . . .

No. If only Ed Smith didn't exist.

Everything would be different then. The weight of the dead man up on Wolf Peak would bear less heavily on him, the fear of exposure would end. Fred knew that Tom Lindahl would never talk about what had happened up there; Tom wasn't the problem. But how could they trust Ed Smith, how could they be sure what he would or would not do next?

The problem wasn't Fred's imagination, that was just inflamed for now by what had happened. The problem wasn't George, who, of course, would be coming home in a year, less than a year, and, of course, Fred would be here to greet him. The problem wasn't Fred or George or Tom or that poor wino up on Wolf Peak.

The only problem was Ed Smith.

After all that thinking, when Fred finally did get to his feet and walk to the bedroom, he did it with almost no conscious thought at all. There was nothing to think about when you were sure, and Fred was sure.

He carried the rifle loosely in his right hand, grasping the warm wood of the stock, pleased as always with the feel of the thing. His memories with that rifle, out hunting, had been very good for a long time, and soon they'd be good again.

He knew that Jane, at the very rear of the house, absorbed in her book, wouldn't hear him drive away, but he coasted backward down the driveway, anyway, and didn't start the engine until he'd backed around onto the empty street. The houses all around him were warmly lit with families together for Sunday evening. Very soon he'd be back among them. The rifle on the seat beside him, he drove toward Tom Lindahl's house.

eight

The parrot saw things in black and white. He knew about this place of his, that it was very strong, and that he was very strong within it, and that whenever he thought he might be hungry, there was food in his tray. He was clean and preferred to stand on his swinging bar rather than down at the bottom of the world, even at those rare moments when the bottom of the world was made new, almost shining white and black, crisp, noisy if touched, until he began to drop upon it again.

For movement, rather than down there, he preferred to move among the swinging wooden bar and the rigid vertical black metal bars of the cage. Up and over, sometimes, for no reason at all, his strong talons gripping the bars even directly above his head, giving him, when he arched his neck back and stared with one round black and white eye at the world, this world, a whole new perspective.

There wasn't much in this world, but not much was

needed. With his strong talons and his strong beak, gripping to the metal bars, a taste like inside your brain on his tongue from the bars, he could move around and control everything he needed.

Outside the cage, enveloping it, was another cage, indifferent to him. Below him, on the one side, dim light glowed upward to suffuse that larger cage with soft auras, constantly shifting. Sometimes grating noises came up from there, too, sometimes not. Beyond, over there, a paler, larger, taller rectangular brightness sometimes briefly appeared, when Creatures entered or departed their world, the one beyond his. At other times they made that rectangle and moved through, but there was no extra light.

He had some curiosity about these Creatures, but not much. He studied them when they were present, usually observing one eye at a time, waiting for them to do something to explain themselves. So far, they had not.

Sometimes the parrot slept. He slept on the swinging bar, talons gripping tight, large button eyes closed, coarse green feathers slightly ruffled upward and forward. When he woke, he always knew he had been asleep, and that nothing had happened, and that, now he was awake, it was time to eat and shit, drink and piss, so he did.

Now it was now. Creatures went out, with not much brightness in their rectangle, and leaving no Creatures behind. The shifting lights from below continued, without the noise. Time went by and the parrot slept, suddenly awakened by a racket.

Another Creature had come in, with banging noises and shouting noises. It crossed in front of the bright square, it went into other darknesses and came back, it yelled and yelled, and then it leaned down to stare at the parrot, to stare at that left eye observing it, and yell and yell the same phrase over and over.

The parrot had never spoken. The parrot had never been in a social situation where it seemed the right thing to do was to speak. The main Creature who lived with him, in his cage outside the cage, almost never spoke. It had never occurred to the parrot to speak.

But now this Creature, some unknown foreign Creature, was yelling the same sounds over and over again, and it came to the parrot that he could make those sounds himself. It might be satisfying to make those sounds. He and the Creature could make those sounds together.

So he opened his beak, for the first time ever not to grip a bar, and the first thing he said was a rusty squawk, which was only natural. But then he got it: "Air izzi? Air izzi? Air izzi?"

The Creature reared back. It shrieked. It yelled many different things, too fast and too many and too jumbled for the parrot to assimilate. Then it jabbed the end of a metal rod into the cage, wanting to poke it against the parrot's chest, but the parrot sidestepped it easily on his swinging bar, then clamped his left talon around the long metal rod.

The Creature had not finished yelling. The parrot joined it: "Air izzi? Air izzi?"

The parrot leaned his head down and swiveled it to the right. His left eye looked down the long round tunnel inside the metal rod. "Air izzi? Air izzi?"

The searing white flame came out so fast.

nine

Trooper James Duckbundy was a health nut, which was why he liked to drive with the cruiser's window open. Trooper Roger Ellis would have been just as happy with General Motors air, but Duckbundy was at the wheel this time out, so it was his call.

They were driving to Pooley from Barracks K because some old coot had reported mislaying his weapon, a handgun. Both troopers understood the citizens' right to bear arms and all that, but both sincerely believed the world would be a safer place if idiots didn't own guns. They could understand how a person at almost any age could mislay their car keys or watch, but to lose your piece? That was just the sort of individual, in their opinion, who shouldn't be armed in the first place.

Of the sleepy little towns in the world, Pooley had to be one of the sleepiest. They drove in to few lights and no traffic, and Duckbundy parked in front of the address, a small house lit up like a Christmas tree, the only house in town that seemed to have every last light switched on, interior and exterior. Losing his handgun seemed to have made the householder nervous.

Because Duckbundy was a health nut, which meant his window was open, before he even switched off the engine they both heard the flat serious crack of a shot. Up ahead it came from, and on the other side of the road.

They looked at each other. "That was no handgun," Ellis said.

"It wasn't applause, either," Duckbundy said, and put the cruiser back in gear.

There were no further shots as they eased slowly down the road, but there didn't need to be. It is a crime to discharge a firearm within five hundred feet of a dwelling, and one time will do.

They both peered at the houses on the left, inching along, until Ellis said, "Movement back there."

There was a boarded-up empty house at that point, with a driveway next to it and what looked like a garage in back. Duckbundy braked, swiveled the spotlight, and clicked it on. In the sudden glare, a man down there by the garage, with a rifle in his right hand, was just getting into a black Taurus. Something wet glistened on the barrel of the rifle as the man spun around, glaring into the light, clutching the rifle now with both hands.

Ellis had the microphone in his palm and carried it with

him as he stepped out to the roadway. “Police,” roared the speaker on the cruiser’s roof. “Stop where you are. Lay the weapon down.”

He didn’t. He screamed something, gibberish, something, and then he did bring the rifle up.

Between them, the troopers fired eleven shots. Any three would have done the job.

ten

What do you call a parrot? Does it have to start with "P"? Polly Parrot; Peaches Parrot. Penitentiary Parrot; not good. Greeny Parrot.

There was less traffic tonight, and fewer roadblocks. It seemed to Tom the authorities no longer believed they had the fugitives trapped; they were just going through the motions.

How was Ed going to get there, without a car and without an ally? Or had he somehow phoned someone, while Tom was away from the house, and arranged to meet with another professional like himself, another hard man, who would come with him to Gro-More to help in the robbery? And get what out of it?

Tom's share, of course.

He could still pull over, at any open gas station, and call the state troopers to tell them where they could find one of the men they were looking for. Unless Ed had left the house almost immediately after Tom.

But it didn't matter; he wasn't going to stop. It was too late to change anything now, too late to decide to do something other than this.

Different cars appeared in his rearview mirror, and some passed him because, with all this fretful thinking inside his head, he couldn't keep up to his normal speed, but poked along at probably ten miles an hour below his regular average. There was a gray Volkswagen Jetta in his mirror for miles, somebody else as poky as he was, but then he came to another of the rare roadblocks, and after that pause, the Jetta was gone, and for some miles his mirror was dark.

He next became aware of other traffic when a different car's lights appeared well behind him, coming on fast. This one was pretty much a speed demon, who tailgated Tom a mile or so and then, at the next passing zone, roared on by him like a freight train. In Tom's headlights, as it raced away, he could see it was a black Infiniti, a faster, more powerful car than his, soon out of sight up ahead.

Perry Parrot? Ed Parrot? Madonna Parrot? William G. Dodd Parrot?

What if he doesn't show up? What if, after all this, I get there and I never see Ed Smith again? What if he's gone from my life just as abruptly as he came into it?

There would be a relief in that, but Tom knew it wasn't the right question. The question was, if Ed Smith disappeared, could Tom do it himself, come back with both duffel bags full, take the whole gate from the track on his own, double the secret inside the boarded-up house?

Tom didn't believe it. If he got there, and waited half an hour and Ed never appeared, he knew damn well what he'd do. He'd turn tail. He was still the same gutless wonder he'd always been. He needed Ed Smith to give him a backbone. He hated that he needed the man, but he knew it was true. Even after all this, he wouldn't be able to take the track's money on his own.

Do I want him to show up? Do I want this thing to happen, or do I want an excuse just to go back to my crappy little house and vegetate in there forever? Which do I want, which do I really want?

Like the parrot's name, he just didn't know.

eleven

Suzanne woke to the patter of pebbles on her window. Annoyed, not wanting to be awake, she thought, Who would be pestering me at this hour? What time is it, anyway?

No, it's not pebbles, it's shooting! Guns, shooting.

Suzanne opened her eyes to utter madness. Instead of the silent dark of her own hushed peaceable room, she was seated upright in some harshly angular place of bands of hard glare that sliced down across full crowded banks of blackness. Light above, dark below, black on all sides – a window?

"Oh! My God, what's—"

"Shut up!"

Another shock. The voice was male, low, intense, guttural, and not at all friendly. It silenced Suzanne like a hand clapped against her mouth, long enough for the sharp bite of the boot lace around her wrists to bring memory crashing back, with all its terror and all its humiliation.

How could she not have realized that it was the bank robber they'd run into? She had been just so full of her normal assumption, for so many years, that as she moved through the world she was simply going to be mistreated, or ignored, or dealt with unfairly, that when a man suddenly appeared in front of her to wave a gun around and tie people up like political prisoners, then march off without a single word of explanation, it had somehow been normal, somehow what she'd expected from the world all along, even though on most days nothing remotely like this had ever happened.

And now that it had happened? She'd been so locked up in her own feelings of mistreatment, expectations fulfilled, that it hadn't even occurred to her to wonder who that man might be or why he would act in such a way.

Bank robbers were being hunted all around the countryside, but when this had happened to Suzanne, did she think, bank robbers? No, she thought, now, see what they're doing to me, and it took Brian Hopwood of all people to tell her, not gently, that this time the story wasn't about her, it was about him, about that man, the one who'd tied them up and gone away.

Then, of course, once Brian had explained to her what was actually happening here, she'd felt such belated terror, mixed with such humiliation, that the tension had kept her absolutely silent for hours, afraid to make somehow an even bigger fool of herself. Brian, who never said anything to anybody, anyway, was also silent through all this, until, who knows how much later, the phone had rung, and rung, and rung, and Brian had finally said, "By God, I hope that's Edna, and I hope she's starting to smell a rat."

But then the phone stopped ringing, and Brian said nothing else, and somehow, despite the discomfort, despite the fear, despite the embarrassment, Suzanne had fallen asleep. Asleep! To wake up who knew when, with gunshots somewhere outside.

Finished now. Who was shooting guns? Was the bank robber back, had he decided he should kill them, after all? But it had been so long since he'd gone away; still daylight then. Wouldn't he be miles and miles from here by now, while Suzanne slept like a rag doll on the floor of Brian Hopwood's filthy gas station, wouldn't he be deep into some other badness by now?

She tried a whisper: "Brian."

"Yes." Gruff but not unfriendly.

"Brian, what's going to happen?"

His laugh now was bitter, and not friendly at all. "Well, we're trussed up here like Thanksgiving turkeys. There isn't a thing for either of us to do until somebody decides to look for us."

"But they're shooting out there. Brian? Who's shooting?"

"How would I know?" He was getting really irritated now.

Looking as much for some way to appease him as for

some way out of their trouble, she said, "Would Edna come here?"

"I don't think that was her, on the phone."

Struck by a sudden thought, she said, "You know, it could have been Jack. You know, my grandfather."

"I know who Jack is," Brian said, very testy. "Why would he call me?"

"Looking for me."

"Oh." Brian considered that, then said, "Will he come looking for you?"

"Not after dark."

"Wonderful."

The silence now outside was worse than the gunshots; in the silence, you didn't know where anybody was. Feeling sudden panic, Suzanne shrilly whispered, "Brian, we have to get out of here!"

"Go ahead." Sardonic, unbelieving, unsympathetic; in other circumstances, rude.

Which she ignored. "No, really," she whispered. "I know you can't move in that chair there—"

"Huh."

"But I can move."

"You're tied hand and foot."

"But I can move. Brian, what if I came over there and—"

"How?"

"I don't know, crawled or rolled or something. What difference does it make?"

"All right," he said. "So you're over here."

"I tied that knot on your wrists. I know what I did. I think maybe, I think maybe I could untie it."

"How do you get at it?"

She thought about that. Now that she was awake and oriented, she could see the office more clearly, even though all the illumination came from outside, from the gas pumps and the soda machine and the streetlight. She and Brian were near each other in the front left corner of the room, where no one looking through any window would be able to see them. The chair Brian was in, taped to the floor, was the only furniture near them. Beyond the dark doorway to the service area, Brian's desk hulked like the recently abandoned headquarters of a defeated army. No, not army; a defeated platoon. An armless kitchen chair, a reluctant acknowledgment that there might someday be a customer to accommodate, stood against the wall on the far side of the desk.

She said, "Brian, is that chair on wheels?"

"No, why should it be?"

"I was just wondering."

"Suzanne, let it go. In the morning, they'll find—"

"I can't wait till morning," she said, and realized it was the truth. Now that she was fully awake, she needed a bathroom, and soon. "Let me just try something," she said, though with every movement the need grew more urgent.

"What are you doing?" he asked, testy as ever, as she started hunching herself across the floor toward him.

"Just let me see . . ."

Ankles and wrists tied together, she could only move in strange little lunges, but soon she was where she wanted to be, with her back to Brian, her tied hands down by his ankles, her hunched shoulders against his shins. Exhausted from the effort, she rested her head a minute, until she realized she was resting it against Brian's thigh and that Brian hated that. So she lifted her head, felt around behind her, and at last came to a part of the duct tape holding the screwdrivers as chocks against the floor, to keep the chair from moving.

Now he grew silent again, and she was aware of his head bent as he tried to see what she was doing and whether or not it would get them anywhere. The duct tape clung fiercely to the wooden floor, but finally she felt far enough along it to reach an end, and could yank that upward. Once started, the tape came more readily, and then the screwdriver itself helped, and, out of breath but triumphant, she could whisper, "I got it!"

"It'll take more than one," he said. "But then I'll be able to help."

This shift in him from being testy with her, scornful of her, impatient with her, to someone who could help was instantaneous and unremarked-upon. She simply accepted the offer with a nod and scooted backward a bit more until she could find some duct tape to assault.

The second screwdriver was easier to remove, now that she knew how, and then Brian could move his chair, though only in tiny increments, since his ankles were still tied together and to the chair. "Now what?" he said. "I don't think I can drive this thing through that door."

"Let me bring that other chair over," she said. "If I can get up on it, maybe I can reach the knots on your wrists."

"What good does that do? They're tight, Suzanne, trust me."

"I tied them myself," she said. "Just let me see what I can do."

"Whatever you want," he said, disbelieving her.

She didn't care. Now that she was moving, she was moving. She rolled across the floor, making herself dizzy, but at last bumping into that other chair. Her legs tied together with jumper cable made for a blunt instrument, but with them she could kick the chair away from the wall and around the edge of the desk and over toward Brian, who, astonishingly enough, was doing what he could do to help. That is, he kept shifting his body forward while pressing down and back on the floor with his white socked feet, inching the chair on its casters out away from the corner, where she would find him easier to reach.

Maneuvering them into position wasn't hard, with his back turned to her and the other chair so that, if she were sitting sideways on it, Suzanne would be able to reach Brian's wrists. No, the hard part was for her to get up onto the chair. She did manage to lunge herself up so she was lying facedown across the chair seat, but then could do no more, had no traction anywhere. At last, half-muffled in that position, she said, "Brian, I need your help."

"Sure. What?"

"I have to put my foot in your lap, and you have to not let it get away. I can't get up on this chair unless I can brace against something."

"I don't know," he said. "I don't know what you're trying to do here, but all right. Let's try it. Jesus, Suzanne, try to be a little careful."

"This will be very fast," she promised.

Well, it wasn't, and she was sorry to have to hear him grit his teeth as her right heel bore into his crotch, but she needed that brace to be able to swivel around on the chair seat, first on her side, then faceup, so that then she could pull herself up with her bound hands behind her against the slats of the chair back.

"There!" she said.

"Jesus."

"I'm sorry, Brian. Can you turn a little more away from me?"

"I certainly can."

There was some fumbling involved, but then, behind her, she could feel his thick-fingered hands, and then the wrists, and then the thin strong shoelace.

Yes, those were the knots she'd made, good strong knots that could be slipped if you knew which part you were pulling. Here's a loop, here's an end, here's—

He jumped as though he'd been electrocuted. "What's that? Wait – wait a minute! My hands are loose!"

"Brian, please, please, untie my wrists, please, please—"

"Yeah, wait, let me see what I'm doing here. He didn't make it easy, that sonofa— There!"

"Oh, thank God!" she said, and bent to tear off the jumper cable pinning her ankles.

He was still struggling with the duct tape on his socks. She jumped to her feet, patting the wall. "Lights."

"We've got to be careful when we go out there, Suzanne, we don't know what's—"

"I don't want to go out there," she said, hurrying through the doorway into the dark interior room. "I want the ladies'!"

He called after her, "You'll need the key!"

twelve

Where was Tom going? It didn't make any sense.

Around seven-thirty, Tom Lindahl's Ford SUV had driven away from the little converted garage he lived in and headed south out of Pooley, with Cory and Cal in the Volkswagen Jetta far behind, and an hour later they were all still driving, heading steadily southwest across New York State, away from Pooley and away from Massachusetts, the site of the bank robbery that Ed Smith's money was supposed to be from.

Were Tom and Smith on their way to get the money? What else could they be doing? Cory had more and more questions in his mind about what was going on here, but he didn't want to voice them, afraid Cal would insist on doing something rash, like ramming that vehicle up ahead just to see what would happen. So Cory kept his doubts to himself and just drove, hoping this journey would soon come to an end.

Cory'd had no trouble borrowing the Jetta from his sister. In fact, she'd been so happy at the idea that Cory might get himself a real job – by which she meant white collar, not the factory-floor stuff he and Cal usually did – that he felt guilty lying to her. But he assured himself it was all going to work out fine, and she wouldn't ever have to know the truth, so he wasn't going to worry about it.

What was a little worrying, at least at first, was that, when Cory went back to the diner, Cal had obviously not limited himself to coffee, the way he'd promised. The beer on his breath wasn't as plain as if they'd been in the cab of the pickup together, but you could still smell it. Cory could have said something, but what was the point? Cal would just deny it, that's all, just lie about it and wait for the question to go away.

That was how Cal always handled problems. It wasn't that he was a good liar – in fact, he was a piss-poor liar, unlike Cory, who had a smooth plausibility about himself – but that once Cal took root in a lie, he would never move from it, so why waste your breath?

At first, when they set up in a driveway next to another of Pooley's empty houses, having to keep well away from Tom's place because it was still daylight, Cal had been tensed up and edgy, because of the beer, wanting something to happen right away. His left eye, covered by the black patch, was neutral, but his working eye was staring and agitated, straining to see through walls, around windows. "When are they gonna make their move?"

“We’ll just wait and see.”

“Maybe I oughta go peek in the window.”

“No, we’ll just wait here. We’ll know when they’re going somewhere.”

Cal had to get out and pee then, and that kept him calmed down for a while, but not for long. Three more times he wanted to go over and peek in Tom’s window to see what was going on over there, and three times Cory had to remind him there was nothing those people could do except, sooner or later, leave the house and come out to the road in this direction. Did Cal want to be halfway down their driveway, on foot, when they came out? Of course not. Did he want them to catch him peeking in the window? Definitely not.

As for what they thought was going on, they’d been over all of that more than once, but restless and bored in the car, waiting for something to happen, Cal had to rehash it just once more. “There’s money in it, we know that much for sure,” he said. “Only thing that makes sense. Tom wouldn’t be hanging out with that guy, giving him cover, pretending he used to work with him, if there wasn’t some sort of payoff in there someplace.”

Cory nodded. “That’s what we’re figuring on, anyway.”

“That’s what we’re counting on,” Cal said. “There’s got to be some of that bank robbery money still hid somewhere, or Tom just wouldn’t be fronting for that guy. I mean, that’s a hell of a risk, Cory.”

"Yeah, it is."

"So that's the only reason he's gonna do it. For the money." Cal laughed in a sudden burst. "I don't know about you, Cory, but I could use that money. Better than a job over at that college, anyway."

"Well, I wouldn't mind that, either," Cory admitted.

Cal grinned at him and gave his arm a reassuring pat. "You'll come through," he said. "You're the smart one."

"And you're the funny one."

"Damn hysterical. Why don't I find a phone somewhere and give them a call, just to see what they do?"

"Because," Cory said, "I don't want them thinking about us, or thinking there's anybody at all interested in them, that would keep them from what they mean to do."

"Well, maybe."

"Remember, I'm the smart one."

So Cal laughed at that and relaxed a little more, and they waited in companionable silence. Gradually evening came on, and then, just at that tricky twilight moment when it's very hard to see because it's neither day nor night, here came the Ford out of Tom Lindahl's driveway and turned south, away from them.

"There it is!"

"I see it, Cal. Take it easy."

Cory watched the Ford recede almost out of sight before he started the Jetta and followed, keeping well back. Beside him, Cal, breathing loudly through his mouth, pulled up his shirttail in front and reached down inside to come out with a smallish automatic, the High Standard GI model in .45 caliber.

Cory stared. "What are you doing with that?"

Cal laughed. "Don't leave home without it." He hadn't seemed drunk before this, but now, hours since he'd had that beer, there was a sudden slurry electricity to him as he sat there holding the automatic with both hands.

"Oh, come on, Cal," Cory said. "You never said you were gonna bring that." Up ahead, Tom Lindahl's Ford moved at a slow and steady pace, easy to follow.

"Well, I just knew you'd give me a hard time if I said anything about it," Cal said. "So I figured, I'll just bring it, and then there won't be any argument."

"If we get stopped by a cop—"

"What for? We're doing" – Cal leaned the left side of his head against Cory's upper arm so his right eye could see the dashboard – "forty-five miles per hour. Who's gonna stop us for that?"

"Cal, I don't want to see that thing."

"No, no, you're not gonna see it." Cal leaned forward to put the gun on the floor, then sat back and rested his right foot on it. "See? Just sitting there."

"Is the safety on, anyway?"

"Sure it is. Whada you think?"

"When we talk to those guys," Cory said, "please, Cal, don't start waving that goddam gun around."

"He's the one talking tough, do you remember that? 'You'd be dead now.' Oh, yeah, would I? We'll just have this little fella down here on the floor here, out of sight, out of mind, and if there has to be a little surprise, somewhere down the road, well, guess what, we got one."

"Just leave it there," Cory said.

"It's there."

Somehow the idea of his brother's gun in his sister's car made Cory nervous, as though he'd got himself involved in some kind of serious mistake here somewhere. Cal had bought that goddam thing years ago, in a pawnshop, on a visit to Buffalo, for no reason at all he could ever explain. He'd just seen it and he wanted it, that's all. From time to time, the first year or so, he'd take it out in the woods and practice, shooting at trees or fence posts, but eventually it more or less just stayed in a drawer in his bedroom, barely even thought about. Cory hadn't thought about it for so long it was like something brand-new, a Gila monster or something, when it suddenly appeared in Cal's lap in the car.

All right, let it stay on the floor. If it made Cal feel more secure to have it down there, fine. When it came time, though, to get out of this car, Cory would make damn sure that stupid gun didn't come out with them.

It was a few miles later they saw the bright red and white lights of their first roadblock of the night. Slowing down, Cory said, "Put the damn gun under the seat."

"Right."

Even Cal seemed a little chastened, as he bent down to hide the gun. Cory drove as slowly as he dared, to give Tom a chance to clear the roadblock, then eased to a stop beside the waiting trooper as he reached for his wallet.

The trooper had a long flashlight that he shone first on Cory and then across him on Cal, not quite shining the beam in their eyes. He was the most bored trooper they'd met yet, and he studied Cory's license without saying a word. Cal had the glove compartment open, but the trooper didn't even bother to ask for registration, just handed the license back and used his flashlight to wave them through.

Tom's Ford hadn't gained much ground, was still slowly moving along as though in no hurry to get anywhere in particular tonight. When Cory caught up, and slowed to maintain the same distance as before, Cal said, "What's goin' on, Cory? Is he just out for a drive?"

"I don't know," Cory admitted. "But I just figured out what's out there, down this way."

"Yeah, what?"

"That racetrack where he used to work."

"What? Tom?"

"He worked there for years, and then they fired him for something."

"What the hell would he be going down to that racetrack for?"

"I don't know what they're doing," Cory said. "I mean, there they are, they came out tonight, everything like we thought they'd do, but now I don't get it. They aren't leading us to any money."

"Maybe Tom's helping the guy get away from here."

"At forty-five miles an hour? Besides, he could've done that last night. Or today."

"Get up closer," Cal said. "Let's see what they're up to."

"They're driving," Cory said.

"Come on, Cory, close it up."

"You can't see inside a car at night."

"Close it up, goddammit."

So Cory moved up much closer, not quite tailgating the Ford, and they drove like that awhile, trying to figure it out, getting nowhere. Then, way ahead, Cory saw the lights of the next roadblock and said, "I gotta ease back," just as Cal yelled, "Goddammit!"

"What?" Cory's foot was off the gas, the Jetta slowing, the Ford moving toward the distant roadblock, its brake lights not yet on.

"He's alone in there!"

"What?"

"Pull over here, pull over here, goddammit!"

A closed gas station was on the right. Cory pulled in, drifting past the pumps as he said, "What do you mean, he's alone in there?"

"Tom! I could see those lights down there through his windshield, and he's goddammit alone in the goddam car! Stop!"

Cory stopped. "Then where is he? Maybe he's lying down in back."

"For a roadblock? He isn't there," Cal insisted, and a black car suddenly passed them on their left and angled to a stop across the front of the Jetta. Cal's one eye stared. "What is this?"

The driver of the other car got out, looking over its roof at them, and, of course, it was Ed Smith. Cory reflexively shifted into reverse as Smith took a step down the other side of his car, as though he wanted to come around and talk to them.

Cal didn't give him the chance. All at once he was lunging out of the Jetta, and when Cory turned to him, he had that automatic in his hand. Cory yelled, "Don't!" at the same time Cal yelled some damn thing at Smith and lifted the automatic as though to shoot Smith, and in the same instant Smith laid his own hand on the roof of his car, with something small and black in it that coughed a dot of red flame and Cal went reeling backward, the automatic dropping onto the gas station's concrete.

Cory screamed, and tromped on the accelerator, and the Jetta tore backward past the pumps, the open passenger door not quite hitting them but rocking as though it would come off its hinges, until Cory pounded his foot on the brake and the door slammed.

Ahead of him across the gas station, Smith was striding forward, that gun in his hand down at his side. Cory spun the wheel, shifted into drive, and tore away from there northward, leaving Cal and Smith and the Ford and the roadblock and everything else to shrink and disappear in the rearview mirror.

Absolute panic compelled him to drive hard for three or four minutes on a road with no traffic until he overtook a slow-moving pickup and had to decelerate. As he slowed, the panic receded and clear thought came back, and he knew he had to go take care of Cal. He was the younger brother, but he'd always been the one with brains, the one who went along with Cal's stunts but then – sometimes – got them both out of trouble when things went too far.

Cal was hit. Shot. How bad?

Cory made a U-turn and headed south again, and would have missed the gas station this time if he hadn't seen that roadblock far ahead. But there was the station, and Cory pulled in, went past the pumps to where he'd stopped the last time, and stopped again. Smith and the black car were gone.

Afraid of what he would find, Cory got out of the Jetta and looked around on the right side of the car. Cal's automatic lay on the pavement where it had fallen, but there was nothing else there. No Cal.

Cory got back into the car, put the automatic on the passenger seat, and drove this way and that so he could use the headlights to look at every part of the gas station property. He found nothing.

There was a night-light inside the station office. Cory got out of the Jetta again and looked through the windows there. He looked everywhere. Cal was gone.

thirteen

State Police Captain Robert Modale looked at the artist's rendering of the bank robber, crumpled and greasy from having been in a desk drawer in Brian Hopwood's gas station, and now that he knew the truth, he could see it, he could see that face, the same face as the man he'd talked with just yesterday up in the St. Stanislas parking lot. They'd talked about Lyme disease, and who would have ever guessed he was this fellow all along? The felons a man met up with usually weren't that bold.

Captain Modale was a calm man, not given to extremes of temperament, but even for him this was a moment out of the ordinary. A lesser man might have sworn or punched a wall, but Captain Modale merely clenched his lips and flared his nostrils a little and nodded down at that picture he held in his unshaking left hand and thought, I'll know you next time.

At the moment, eight-fifty on this Sunday evening, the

captain was standing in the brightly lit living room of an old fellow named Jack Riley, whose report of a stolen revolver, a .22-caliber S&W Ranger, had started the unraveling of tonight's events. Riley, bright-eyed and eager, perched on the forward edge of the easy chair where he obviously usually spent his time watching that television set over there. His granddaughter, Suzanne Gilbert, a good-looking woman if a little peremptory in manner, seeming apparently none the worse for wear after having been knocked around and tied up by the bank robber, sat on the arm of the same chair, her right hand protectively on her grandfather's left shoulder. Brian Hopwood, still in his dirty work clothes, stood beside the sofa, talking on Riley's phone to his wife, explaining to her all that had happened and reassuring her, possibly, that everything was all right now. Trooper Oskott stood at semi-attention over by the front door.

They were all waiting for Captain Modale to sort things out and decide what to do next, but by God, there was a full dossier here of things to sort out. There were too many people in this incident, it seemed to the captain, and too many relationships.

Start with the bank robber, who everyone here had known as Ed Smith, a name that had produced thousands of results upon the captain inputting it into the onboard computer in the cruiser, none of them seeming to be helpful in any way. So start with Mr. Ed Smith, whose name was certainly not Ed Smith, but who, for convenience's sake, would be given that name, at least for now. What were the relationships between Smith and the other people in Pooley – or Fred Thiemann, too, let's not forget the fellow just recently shot down by the captain's own officers just across the road there – and how deep and long-standing might those relationships have been?

On entering this room, after being driven down here by Trooper Oskott from Barracks K, greeting the people already assembled here by the troopers who'd been the first responders to Jack Riley's complaint, the captain had dropped onto the dark wood coffee table in front of the sofa the yellow legal pad he'd brought along with him, so that he could accept the Wanted poster Hopwood insisted on handing him, and now he sat down on the sofa facing that pad, Riley and the Gilbert woman to his right, television set to his left, Hopwood standing at the end of the sofa to his left, and took a retractable pen from his pocket. Clicking it open after putting the Wanted poster under the legal pad, he said, "I'd like first to close with this fellow Smith, and everybody's relationship with him."

Suzanne Gilbert, as though she might become offended, said, "Relationship? None of us had a relationship with that man."

"I never even met him," Jack Riley added.

Brian Hopwood, just off the phone, pulled over the small wooden chair from beside the television set, sat on it as though afraid to make it dirty, and said, "I only saw him that one time in my life, this afternoon, when he came in for gas."

"But you recognized him."

"Not right away. But I thought about it, and when he came back in to get his change – he didn't use up the cash he gave me – I had it doped out who he was, and I went ahead and did one of the dumbest things I've ever done in my life."

"You did exactly what a good citizen should have done, under the circumstances," the captain told him, though he himself didn't believe it even while he was saying it.

Nor did Hopwood. "A good citizen with a death wish," he suggested.

The captain decided to let that drop. Facing the others, he said, "So none of you had had dealings with this man before today."

With seeming reluctance, as though still troubled by that word "relationship," Suzanne Gilbert said, "Well . . . I saw him last night."

"Ah," the captain said, not showing his surprise. "And where was that?"

"Just outside there," she said, nodding at the front window. "I was driving by, and he was walking along the road. You don't usually see people walking around here."

"No," the captain agreed. "You just happened to be driving by?"

"No, I often drive this way after work," she said, as

though he'd accused her of something and she was determined to rise above it. "If Jack wants to talk, he'll have the porch light on."

"Ah. And was the porch light on?"

"No, it wasn't."

"I was asleep in front of the damn TV," Riley said. "Again."

"And you saw this man," the captain said. "Just walking, you say?"

"Yes. I thought it was strange, so I stopped and asked him if I could help with anything, and he said he was staying with Tom Lindahl—"

"The man whose parrot was shot."

She looked blank. "I'm sorry?"

So these people hadn't heard that part of it. "Nothing," the captain said, not wanting a distraction.

But Hopwood said, "Somebody shot a parrot?"

"Tom Lindahl's parrot."

"I never knew he had one," Hopwood said. "Why would anybody shoot a parrot?"

"To keep it from talking," Jack said, and actually cackled.

"Jack!" his granddaughter said, reproving him, and squeezed his shoulder to make him behave.

To her, the captain said, "Let's get back. This man you talked to last night said he was staying with Tom Lindahl."

"Yes." She looked a little confused and said, "So then I thought it was all right."

Hopwood said, "He had Tom's car, at the station, I know that car."

Suzanne Gilbert said, "Did he do something to Tom, too?"

"We don't know, ma'am," the captain said. "He isn't at home, and neither is his car."

Hopwood said, "That fellow stole Jeff Eggleston's car. From my place."

"The black Infiniti," the captain said. "Yes, I know, we've put out a bulletin on it."

"What I mean is," Hopwood said, "if he's got Jeff's car, he can't have Tom's. You can only drive one car."

"Then we have to assume," the captain said, "that Lindahl is driving his own car. Does anybody have any idea where he might go?"

"Nowhere," Hopwood said, and Suzanne Gilbert said, "When I talked to that man last night, he said Tom Lindahl was a hermit. I think that's true."

The captain paused, trying to think of a question that might help him move forward on this problem, and in the little silence the front doorbell rang, startling them all. The captain said, "Trooper Oskott can answer."

The trooper turned, opened the door, and spoke briefly with somebody on the porch. Then he turned back to say, "To see you, Captain."

"Thank you." Rising, he told the others, "I think we're just about finished. Let me see what this is."

"I'd like to get home," Hopwood said.

"I'm sure you would," the captain said, and went out to the porch, where a plainclothes state police inspector named Harrison said, "How's it going?"

"Confusing."

"Well, this may help a little. Mrs. Thiemann gave us a statement."

"Yes?"

"She says her husband was part of the group that went out looking for the fugitives yesterday."

"I saw them there," the captain said. "He was teamed up with the missing householder here, Lindahl, and this fella we've been calling Smith."

"She says, her husband told her, they went up to Wolf Peak—"

"That's right."

"And up there her husband shot and killed a man."

Now the captain could not hold his astonishment. "He did what?"

"Some old wino, bum, something like that." Harrison shrugged. "He got excited, Thiemann, he thought it was one of the bank robbers, and shot him."

"I swear I don't understand this situation," the captain said. "One of them's a bank robber, another of them suddenly ups and kills a man – and a parrot – and the third, an ordinary fellow his entire life, goes missing."

"The thing is," Harrison said, "Thiemann would have

turned himself in, but Smith talked him out of it, said it was to protect Thiemann."

"It was to protect Smith."

"Well, sure. But Thiemann couldn't stand it. His wife said it drove him crazy."

The captain looked across the road. "So he came down here to confront Smith. Nobody home."

"Lucky for Lindahl," Harrison said, and corrected himself. "Lucky for somebody."

"This Smith," the captain said, "robs a bank in Massachusetts, escapes, gets this far, hooks up with two other people, ordinary people, everybody starts going nuts."

Harrison said, "You think he did it to them, somehow?"

"I truly don't know," the captain said, and looked out from the lighted porch at the dark road. "We are not going to know," he said, "what this is really all about until Tom Lindahl tells us. I do wish I could lay my hands on him." He nodded at the darkness. "Yes, Lindahl," he said, "I would really like to know where you are."

fourteen

Around nine-thirty, Bill Henry yawned, stretched, pushed back from the desk where his latest Field & Stream had lain open and unread for some time now, and got to his feet. One more yawn and he said, “I think I’ll walk around a little.”

Max Evanson, his usual partner on the overnight shift, looked up from his People magazine in some surprise: “Walk around what?”

“The track. The building. Just around.”

Max still didn’t get it. A traditional kind of guy, who only believed in, as he’d said more than once, “meat and potatoes,” he wouldn’t see any reason for Bill or himself or anyone else on night guard duty at Gro-More to get up from his comfortable chair in security unless his shift was over. He said, “You’re gonna walk around the track? It’s, what, it’s two miles, mile and a half, something like that.”

“I’m not going to walk around the track,” Bill said. “That’s not what I mean at all. Look, Max, I'm outa here the middle of next month, just in time for Thanksgiving, I'm feeling a little different about the place, okay? You get it?"

"No," Max said.

"I've been working here thirty-seven years," Bill said, "the last five in this dumb security office, and pretty soon I'm not gonna be working here any more."

"I'm fourteen months behind you," Max said, as though it were a prayer.

"Well, fourteen months from now, you'll feel the same way I do," Bill assured him.

"And what's that?" The skepticism twanged in Max's voice.

"Not nostalgic exactly—"

"Nostalgic! For this place? The people running this outfit here—"

"No, not nostalgic," Bill insisted. "It's just— You spend so much of your life at a place, you know you're gonna leave it, you won't really miss it, but still you want to fix it in your mind before you go."

"It's fixed in my mind," Max promised him.

"Well, I'm gonna take a little walk around," Bill said. "Mind the store."

"Huh," Max said.

The way it was set up, because of insurance and getting people bonded and all that, security at Gro-More had been a special set-off company since just after World War Two. The track contracted for security arrangements from that company, everything from staff for crowd control to spy cameras, and the employees of the subcompany shared in the not-very-good health and pension benefits available to the rest of the track's workforce.

For most of his thirty-seven years here, Bill Henry had been assigned crowd control out by the entrance gates, and he'd enjoyed it. It was pleasant out in the air, and more interesting than the occasional stint in front of the betting windows, showing the uniform and the holstered sidearm and looking stern, just as though there was a chance in hell one of these bettors would suddenly up and rob the place. Never happen.

So what they did with the security employees, as they got older, nearer retirement, less intimidating out in public regardless of the brown uniform and the holstered firearm, was move them to the overnight guard detail. A simple, easy life if you liked to read, which most of the guys did. A short workweek, reduced pay, but retirement was right out there at the end of it, so not really a problem.

Parts of the track were kept locked at night, like the money room downstairs and the tellers' cages upstairs, but most of the rest of it inside the security wall was open, illuminated just enough to satisfy the fire code. Leaving the office now, Bill walked first down the corridor past more offices and then out to the rail near the finish line, down to his right. The main dirt course was a long oval under the dim lights, extending left and right, with the slightly smaller turf course a green river within, and then the interior lawn, a different green, with its ornamental fountain and some perennial flowers that were starting at this time of year to give up the ghost.

At night, empty, the track looked much bigger than in the daytime, as though it could probably be seen from the moon, though he knew that was impossible. Bill liked the size of it at night, and the emptiness of it, and the fact that, in all that big empty space, there was never even one echo. It was as though the track absorbed sound, making the place restful and eternal and also just a little spooky.

He made his way leftward along the rail to the far turn, where a lane would lead down to the paddocks if he felt like going there, but he thought he better not. There were always a few of the grooms and assistant trainers sleeping somewhere near their animals, on cots or in sleeping bags, because this horse or that was having some kind of problem, and those people didn't like other humans around to spook their beasts.

Bill turned away, walking toward the end of the clubhouse and grandstand, all in one building, and as he walked, he saw the reflection of headlights sweep over the white wooden wall that enclosed the entire track area.

Headlights? They were outside, so he couldn't see them directly, only their glow above the wall, and as he stopped to frown at that unexpected aura, the lights switched off.

But what were they doing here? Nobody was supposed to be in that area beyond the wall at night. That would be where the service road came in, at the end of the clubhouse, and there was never any reason for traffic out there after the track shut down.

Unless it was somebody out to harm the horses.

Why that should be, Bill had never understood, but there was a kind of sick human being who just liked to mutilate horses. Attack them with knives, axes, bottles of acid.

Why would people do things like that? They were always caught, drooling and bloody, and they were always put away in a nuthouse somewhere, and there was never any explanation. Whatever went wrong in your life, whatever went wrong in your head, why take it out on a horse?

And is that what he'd happened across tonight? It was those sickos, he knew, who primarily made his job as a night guard here at the track necessary, that and the constant fear of fire. So is that what he'd found, some maniac with a chain saw in his fist? Was he about to become a hero, like it or not?

He thought the thing to do was go back into the clubhouse and walk around to where he could look out one of the windows facing the service road. Let's just see what's out there. Couldn't hurt.

fifteen

Tom Lindahl drove past the main entrance to Gro-More, with its outlined stylized bulls on the gates, then drove on past the dirt road, unmarked except for the Dead End sign, that he should have taken down to the end of the clubhouse. But he just kept driving.

For a mile or two, he didn't even think about what he was doing, but just drove on as though that were his only purpose in being out here, to drive aimlessly, forever. It was easy, and it was comforting, and it didn't make any sense.

After a couple of miles, he came to himself enough to realize this wasn't going to work. He hadn't seen Smith anywhere on the long drive down, he'd come to believe he'd never see Smith again, but that didn't mean he could just drive on and on. Where to? For what?

I can't go back, he thought for the very first time.

That was a chilling thought. He was on a dark country road, and up ahead there was an intersection with a lit-up diner on the right. Refusing to think, clenching his teeth to hold back the floodgates of thought, he waited till he reached the diner, pulled in, stopped in the semidark around at the rear, opened his window, and shut off the engine. Then he slumped and stared at the back of the building, the Dumpster, the screen door closed over the glaringly bright kitchen.

I can't go back there. He meant Pooley, he meant the little converted garage he'd been living in, he meant that whole life.

He didn't think, I can't go home. That wasn't home, he hadn't had a home for years. That was where he'd camped out, waiting for something to happen, although, until Smith had come along, there was never anything going to happen except one day he wouldn't be waiting any more.

But Smith had come along and riled up the waters. Tom had met him, and hooked up with him, and told him about this racetrack opportunity, because he'd thought he wanted revenge and money, but he'd been wrong. He'd wanted a hand grenade to throw into the middle of his empty unbearable life, and boy, he'd sure found one.

He couldn't go back because too many people had seen him with Smith, and, one way or another, who Smith really was would be bound to come out. If somehow they went ahead with this robbery, the police would automatically look at Tom Lindahl, simply because he was a former employee with a grudge, and what would they find? The mysterious Ed Smith, come and gone at just the exact right moment.

But even without the robbery, how long would Smith's identity stay hidden? Fred Thiemann suspected something, though he wasn't sure yet just what it was. Fred's wife, Jane, was smarter and more persistent than Fred, and if she started to wonder about Smith, that would be the end of it. And weren't Cory and Cal Dennison poking their noses in somehow?

So the only thing for Tom to do was what he'd instinctively started to do. Just drive, keep driving south, try to find somebody else to be, somebody else in some other place. Smith had told him it was impossible to disappear like that today, but that couldn't be true. People vanished. And God knows, if there was one thing Tom Lindahl wanted to do, it was vanish.

The only question was, should he go back to the track, just to see if Smith showed up? Without Smith, he knew he wouldn't be doing any robbery here tonight, wouldn't even go into the clubhouse, wouldn't even get out of the car. But at least he should go back, look at Gro-More one last time before closing that part of his life at last. He'd give Smith, say, half an hour, then drive away from here and never be Tom Lindahl again.

Once the decision was made, it was easy, as though it had always been easy; he'd just been too close to it to see the path. Now he could see it. He started the engine, drove back to

Dead End, and this time headed on in. He went to where there was the right turn to the chain-link fence, and stopped at the gate there. He didn't get out of the car but looked through the fence at the clubhouse and after a minute switched off the headlights. He didn't need them to know where he was.

Smith, in the dark beside Tom's open window, said, "Time to get started."

part four

one

Parker saw the gray Volkswagen Jetta start out of Pooley after Tom Lindahl's Ford SUV, and fell in line behind it, in the Infiniti he'd taken from Brian Hopwood's gas station. The best opportunity to deal with the Jetta and the two inside it came just before the second roadblock, when the Jetta pulled off onto the apron of a closed gas station. Parker stopped beside them, planning to talk to them, see what he had to do to get rid of them, maybe shoot their tires out or shoot up their ignition, whatever it would take to scare them off, but before he got close enough to say anything, the idiot Cal was out of the Jetta and waving a handgun around and Parker put him down.

The other one got scared, all right, and skittered away from there like a drop of water on a hot frying pan, but Parker knew he'd be back. Cory'd made it his lifework to stand with his dumber crazier brother, so once the fright wore off, he'd have to come back.

The only problem was the body. Without the body, Cory would have nothing to say to the troopers down there at the roadblock, too far for them to have heard the flat crack of Parker's single shot. The troopers were more bored tonight, less convinced they'd find anything useful out here, and they weren't searching cars, not even cars with two males inside, so Parker threw the body into the trunk, went through the roadblock without a problem, flashing the Infiniti's registration he'd found in the packet with the owner's manual, plus William G. Dodd's driver's license, and a few miles later, at a silent dark empty stretch of road, no buildings in sight, he dumped the body off the road and down a slope toward a chattering little creek he could hear but not see.

Shortly after that, he overtook the SUV, still potting along ten miles below the speed limit. He passed it when he could, and went on to the track, leaving the Infiniti on the scrub ground outside the chain-link fence away to the left of the road, facing back toward the gate. Then he switched off the engine, buttoned the overhead light not to turn on when the door was opened, and waited.

It took longer than it should have for Tom to get there. Had he lost his nerve? If he was running, too spooked to think what best to do for himself, Parker would have no choice but to drive away from here and forget the track. He couldn't get in without Tom's keys and Tom's knowledge.

Without Tom, he'd just drive south through the night. No profit from the bank in Massachusetts, and now no profit from this racetrack. In the morning, wherever he was, he'd phone Claire to drive out and get him, and that would be the end of it. It had been too long since he'd seen her.

But here was Tom. Parker saw the headlights coming down the dirt road and got out of the Infiniti. Walking toward the gate as the SUV drove to it and stopped, he saw Tom in the amber glow from the dashboard, his window open, Parker coming to him from that side.

Tom just sat there, not aware of Parker, but then at last he switched the ignition off, and in the darkness Parker said, "Time to get started."

two

Parker carried the duffel bags, still folded into their plastic wrap, and followed Lindahl through the same routine as last time, first punching the code into the alarm box beside the gate, then keying the gate open so he could drive the Ford in to stop at the closed top of the ramp that led down to the safe room. Getting out of the Ford there, as Parker walked up to him, he looked back at the fence and said, "Do you have a car here?"

"We'll get to it later. We want to be in and out of this."

"Sure. Fine."

Once again Lindahl keyed them into the building and led them among the rooms through the same route around the spy cams. This time there was no leftover food in the accounts department to be knocked over, and no sign of the mess they'd made before. At the end, Lindahl waited for that camera in the corridor to start its sweep away from them, then they strode down to the stairwell door and inside. Down one flight, Lindahl pressed his face to the small window in the door there, to see where this camera was in its cycle, then led them out and to the door at the end of this corridor, the key already in his hand.

Once again, when the door closed behind them, they were in full dark. Parker knew Lindahl was afraid the camera outside would be able to see light through the small window in this door here, so he waited in the darkness, holding the packages of duffel bag and pressing one elbow back against the closed door to keep his orientation.

Out ahead was the sound of Lindahl's scuffing feet as he moved cautiously toward the door they wanted. There was a little silence, then the sound of the key in the lock and the door opening, and at last the ceiling fluorescents clicked on in the safe room off to the right, so Parker could see this outer room with the forklift truck in the corner and the windowless garage door at the far end.

There were two pallets of the money boxes on the floor in here tonight. Lindahl, a nervous grin flickering on his frightened-looking face, said, "Double our money, huh?"

"That's what we're doing. Here."

He handed one of the duffel bags to Lindahl, who took it and said, "How do you want to work this?"

"We open the boxes and put the cash in the bags. Don't bother with singles and fives."

"No, I meant, how do we divide this?"

Parker shook his head. "We aren't gonna divvy it up," he said. "What you put in the bag, you carry home."

"Fine."

They started to strip the plastic off the duffel bags, and a glaring light snapped on in the next room. They stopped, looking at each other, and a voice out there called, "Anybody here?" The voice tried to sound in control, but there was a quaver in it.

Parker handed the duffel to Lindahl and pointed at the corner behind the open door as he started toward that doorway, calling, "Hello? How do I get out of here?"

Behind him, Lindahl moved silently into the corner, his face drained of blood, and Parker stepped through to the outer room, where he saw, over by the door they'd come in, a guy in a brown guard uniform. He was big, maybe six and a half feet, and once brawny, but now out of condition, older and too long comfortable. In the glare of the overhead fluorescents, his eyes and cheekbones showed fear. He was armed with a revolver, but it wasn't in his hand, it was still in its holster on his right hip, and his right hand was still on the light switch just to the right of the door.

Now, seeing Parker, he lowered that hand to the butt of the revolver but didn't unsnap the safety strap that held it in the holster. He patched over the fear with a deep frown and said, "What the hell you doing here?"

"Trying to get out." Parker looked back over his shoulder at the safe room. "What kind of place is that?"

"What do you mean, trying to get out of here?" The guard, not sensing threat, had settled into the indifferently bullying tactic that would always have been his method with civilians.

Parker spread his hands. “Everything’s locked. I can’t get out of the goddam place.”

“That’s kept locked,” the guard told him, jutting his jaw toward the safe room.

“No, it wasn’t,” Parker said. “I saw the light in there, maybe it’s a way out at last.”

“I don’t get this,” the guard said. “What are you doing in here? The end of the day, every day, there’s a sweep, make sure everybody’s out.”

“I fell asleep,” Parker said. “In the men’s room, in a stall.” He didn’t try to act embarrassed, just matter-of-fact. “I didn’t have that much to drink. I been working double shifts for a while now . . .” He shrugged it off. “Can you get me out of here?”

The guard was suspicious, but he wasn’t sure of what. Nodding at the safe room, he said, “That door’s kept locked.”

“It was open, just like that,” Parker told him, pointing at the doorway. “Door hooked open and the lights on. You think I got keys to this place? Look at the door, I didn’t bust in, it was just like that. Listen, I’m sorry. If you wanna call the cops on me, go ahead, but I just gotta get out of here.”

The guard considered him. “We’ll go to the office,” he decided.

“If that’s on the way out,” Parker said, “fine.”

“You lead the way.”

"Sure. But you'll have to tell me which way I'm leading."

The guard's right hand went from the revolver butt to the doorknob behind him. Opening the door, stepping to one side, he said, "Just go out and down the hall."

"Sure."

As Parker went by him, the guard frowned at the door he was holding. "Was this unlocked, too?"

"No, it wasn't shut."

"It's always shut."

Parker waited while the guard followed him out and pulled the door closed. "It wasn't like that," he said. "It was almost shut, but not all. I could just push it. And I saw those lights in there."

"Something's funny here," the guard said, and nodded at the corridor. "Just go straight down."

"Right."

They walked past the door on the left leading to the stairwell that Parker and Lindahl had used. Parker didn't look that way but faced straight, and at the end the guard directed him to turn left down a different corridor. This was a completely different route from the one he'd taken before with Lindahl, and it led finally to an elevator. So this guard didn't like climbing stairs.

He also didn't like being in the enclosed space of the metal elevator with Parker. He stood against the back wall, hand on the revolver butt again, this time his fingers toying with the safety strap as he looked sidelong at Parker.

At the top, the corridor was carpeted. "To the left."

They walked down the corridor, Parker in front, and the guard said, "The open door on the right."

"What?" Somebody past that open door had heard the voice.

Parker made the turn, and this was the security room, with banks of television monitors, shotguns locked into racks on the wall, and several desks, only one of them occupied, by a slightly smaller version of the first guard, equally out of shape.

This one started to rise when he saw Parker, then settled back again when his partner came in. Looking at the partner, he said, "Bill? Whatchu got here?"

"He was in the safe room."

"He what?" Now he did get up from the desk and frowned at Parker but kept talking to his partner. "What's he doing in there?"

"Says he's trying to find the way out. Says he went asleep in the john." Pointing at the monitors, he said, "You see him on any of the screens?"

"I saw you, that's all." Now he did speak to Parker: "How'd you get in there?"

"Walked."

He didn't like that. "Don't get snotty with me, fella."

"I told this guy," Parker said with a gesture at Bill, "I fell asleep, I woke up, I'm trying to get out of here. Everything's locked."

"Except the safe room," said Bill. "How d'ya like that?"

"I don't," the second one said, and to Parker he said, "You got anybody with you?"

"I didn't see anybody," Bill said.

"When I sleep in the men's room," Parker said, "I sleep alone."

The second one was getting steamed. He glared at Parker a long minute, then said, "I may have to tenderize you."

"We'd better call the troopers," Bill said.

"We'll get to that," his partner said. Still glaring at Parker, he pointed at the top of his desk and said, "Empty your pockets."

"Sure." Parker took the automatic out of his pocket and showed it to them as he stepped to the left, so he could see them both. "Is this good enough?"

"God damn you—" The second one was red-faced now and angrier than ever. He moved as though to come around the desk.

"Max! Jesus, Max, fourteen months, remember?"

That stopped Max, or at least slowed him down. "What a hell of a thing you brought me," he said.

Parker said, "On the floor, both of you, over there. Facedown."

Neither moved. Max said, "There's two of us."

"There could be none of you. You go on the floor without a bullet in you, or you go on the floor with a bullet in you. Now."

"Fourteen months, Max," Bill said, and, stiffly lowered himself to the floor, having trouble getting down, and then having more trouble rolling onto his stomach.

Max watched him, tense, not wanting the humiliation in front of this armed stranger, but finally realized there was no choice. He tried to be more graceful getting down, but failed, and finally lost his balance and landed on his bottom with a thump. Quickly, then, he scrambled around to lie prone, turning his face away.

Parker said, "Where do you keep the cuffs?"

"Fuck you," Max told the carpet.

Parker said, "I may have to tenderize you, friend."

Bill said, "They're in the desk with the flowerpot on it, bottom side drawer."

Parker found them and tossed them onto the floor between the two guards. "Bill, you put them on Max."

Max was muttering, "Goddammit, goddammit, goddammit," but he stopped when he sensed Bill getting up onto his knees. They all waited to see what Bill would do, which for a few seconds was nothing.

Parker said, "That's far enough up, Bill. Do it."

Bill was sheepish. "Sorry, Max," he said as he clipped the cuffs onto the other man's wrists, behind his back.

"How do we let him do this, goddammit?"

"He's got the gun, Max."

"So do we!"

"His is in his hand."

"Facedown, Bill," Parker said, and quickly cuffed him, then placed two chairs between the men's legs, to keep them from rolling over or moving around. With a last look at all the empty corridors and rooms on the monitor screens, he headed fast for the elevator.

three

Lindahl sat on the duffel bags, both of them full. The money trays were scattered around the open boxes, still full of small bills and coins. Lindahl seemed to be thinking hard, and it took him a second to realize Parker had come back. Then, startled, he jumped to his feet and said, "Is it me now?"

Parker looked at him. "Is what you?"

"I knew that guy," Lindahl said. "I recognized the voice. He worked here forever. His name's Bill."

"That's right."

"Big man. I've been trying to remember his last name."

Parker said, "You filled the bags. That's good."

Looking down at them, Lindahl said, "I tried to make it as even as I could, between them. If it matters."

"So now you unlock us out of here."

Lindahl didn't move. He kept gazing at the duffel bags, as though still trying to remember Bill's last name, then looked sidewise at Parker and said, "You killed him, didn't you?"

"No," Parker said. "Why would I have to?"

"I brought you here, I brought you into all this. But you don't belong in this— with these people. I keep thinking about Fred."

Parker needed to get out of here, but Lindahl was going through some sort of crisis and would have to be waited out. "What about Fred?"

"He's going crazy. He killed that man, and it's driving him crazy."

"I think he was a little crazy before that," Parker said. "Maybe because of his son, or I don't know what. He killed a man who wasn't a threat to him or anybody else."

"He should have turned himself in. It was only to save you."

"It would have been bad for him to turn himself in. It wouldn't make him less crazy to wind up doing time."

"It wouldn't be on his conscience now," Lindahl said, "and that man wouldn't be up . . . They'd find his family. He'd get a burial."

"Maybe. Tom, what we have to do now is get these bags out of here, and then it's all over."

"If you killed Bill," Lindahl said, "you'll kill me, too."

"Tom," Parker said, "you don't kill somebody unless you have to. It puts the law on you like nothing else. Worse than what we've been having."

"Where is he?"

Parker frowned at him. This was taking too long. "Bill is

handcuffed on the floor in the security office, along with the other one, Max."

"You had handcuffs?"

"The security office had handcuffs. Tom, snap out of this now. We've got to get out of here."

Lindahl looked toward the door, as though he meant to go to the security office, to see for himself if his old friends Bill and Max were alive in there, but then he shook his head and said, "You get to imagine different ways, different ways it can go."

"The way it's going," Parker said, "we get out of here now."

Lindahl took a deep breath. "You're right," he said, and moved toward the doorway, taking keys from his pocket.

four

Parker waited in the safe room doorway as Lindahl carried his keys to the alarm box beside the garage door at the end of the corridor. One key opened the box, and a second switched off the alarm.

This was the alarm that would have made it necessary for them to come back down here after removing the money, shutting the door from the inside and reactivating the alarm, then retracing their route to the other door, so that a light wouldn't flash in security. Now that Parker had had to deal with the guards in security, it didn't matter any more if that light flashed on. A simpler operation but more hurried.

Lindahl, finished with the alarm, opened the garage door, and there was the ramp, leading upward to ground level, where his Ford waited beyond the locked chain-link gate. Parker watched Lindahl start up the ramp to get his car, then he turned back to pick up one of the duffel bags and carry it out of the safe room. When he reached the outer room, Lindahl was back, too soon, without the car and looking worried.

"Something wrong," he said, half a whisper.

Parker put the duffel on the floor. "What?"

"There's another car up there," Lindahl said. "A gray car. It's backed up against the rear bumper of my Ford. I don't see anybody in it."

"No, he's not in it," Parker said. "If he backed his car against yours, that's so he can watch the driver's side. He's up there on the left somewhere, in the dark, in a place where he can watch both the door where we came in and the driver's side of his car. We have to go one way or the other to get out of here, and he knows it."

"But who?" Lindahl peered at Parker as though it had become harder to see him. "Do you know who it is?"

"Cory Dennison."

"Cory! What the hell's he doing here?"

"Looking for our money." Parker took a step toward the ramp but didn't go up it.

Lindahl said, "Isn't Cal with him?"

"No, it's just Cory, but that's enough."

Lindahl shook his head. "Cory and Cal are always together, they don't do things on their own."

"This time," Parker said, "it's just Cory."

Lindahl stared at him, trying to frame some question. Parker waited for him, then said, "Is there something you want to know?"

Lindahl thought about it, looking more worried than ever. Then he said, "There was a car behind me, for a while, might have been that one. Was that Cal and Cory?"

"Yes."

"Together then, but just Cory now. Is Cal waiting somewhere else?"

"No."

Lindahl nodded and looked away. Parker said, "What our problem is, he's got us boxed in down here. We can't waste a lot of time on this. If one of those guards has a wife that likes to call him late at night, what happens when she doesn't get an answer?"

Lindahl stopped worrying about Cal and turned to look up the ramp. "You're right. If I go up there and push his car with mine . . ."

"His car is in gear with the emergency brake on. You know that's what he's going to do. The minute you start your engine, he'll shoot you."

"But we have to get out of here."

"We will. The gate's unlocked?"

"Yes, but it's still closed. I was unlocking it when I saw the other car."

"Turn off the lights down here," Parker said, "and sit tight."

He started toward the ramp, but Lindahl said, "Wait."

"What is it?"

"What if . . ." Lindahl gestured vaguely at the ramp.

"What if Cory comes down, instead of me?"

"Yes."

Parker nodded at the door to the corridor. "Go that way. You've got keys, lock doors behind you."

"My car."

"The guards have pistols," Parker told him. "Get one and do your best. Lights out."

"Right."

As Lindahl switched off the lights, he was looking at that inner door.

five

Pistol in his hand, Parker went up the ramp in the darkness, stopping by the closed gate to wait for his eyes to adjust. There was no moon right now, but many high stars that gave the world a slight velvet gray illumination. Beyond the chain-link gate, he could see the bulk of Lindahl's black SUV and beyond that the gray Jetta. A number of parked track vehicles were an indistinct mass to the left, along the wall beyond the end of the clubhouse. To left and right, the wall curved away into darkness.

Parker knew this area was a large enclosed trapezoid with this end of the clubhouse as its narrow edge, and eight-foot-high wooden walls curving out from it to meet the main wooden wall that surrounded the property. Inside the wall, there was nothing but grass and dirt, except for those vehicles parked to the left. So that's where Cory would be.

There was no way to be silent when opening the gate. A U-shaped metal bar had to be lifted out of the way. The noise it made was small but sharp; Cory would have heard it.

The gate was built in two sections, hinged at the far sides. Parker pulled open the right side just far enough so he could slip through, then went to the ground in front of the Ford and made his way, prone, leftward past the car, then straight out toward those parked vehicles, crawling forward with the gun out ahead of himself. If he were to move to left or right, there was a chance Cory could see his movements against the white wall or the white end of the clubhouse. As long as he kept that bulk of the two cars and the gate behind him, there'd be nothing to make him a silhouette.

The world was absolutely silent, except for the tiny scuffing sounds he made as he moved across the weedy ground. Then, out ahead, he heard a metallic click, and an instant later a pair of headlights flashed on.

It was some sort of big vehicle, the headlights higher than on a car, pointed at an angle to his right, but with plenty of leftover glare to show him on the ground, midway between the trucks ahead and the gate behind.

Parker shot the nearer headlight, then rolled to his right, closer to the beam, as he heard an answering shot from out in front and the smash of a car window behind him. Prone again, he shot out the second headlight, then rolled back to his left as Cory fired twice more, still shooting too high, the way most people do when they're firing at something below them.

Cory didn't waste any more ammunition. Parker got his elbows underneath himself, then pushed up to his feet and ran forward at a crouch. The headlights had spoiled his night vision for a few seconds, but they would have done the same for Cory.

The rear doors of an ambulance. The vehicle with the headlights had been facing outward and was down to the right. Parker moved around the left side of the ambulance, came to the wall beyond it, and stopped. He looked left and right but saw nothing against the wall. He waited and listened.

Silence. Cory was still in here somewhere, in this collection of vehicles. If he was smart, he'd stay in one place and wait for Parker to move, knowing Parker would have to move, he couldn't still be stuck in here at daybreak.

Cory wouldn't have been inside the vehicle with the lights but would have reached in through an open side window to switch them on. Probably he'd had to stand on an exterior step of the thing, which was why it had been a few seconds before he'd started firing, the time he'd needed to step back down to the ground.

Would he still be over there, near that vehicle? Had he seen Parker's run? Would he have any idea where Parker was now?

Time to move. Keeping his back against the wooden wall, Parker sidled leftward. Next past the ambulance was a pickup truck, also facing this way, then a two-wheeled horse trailer tilted forward, and then a small fire engine, facing out.

Was this the thing with the lights? The next vehicle was another pickup, facing outward, but too small to be the one with those lights.

Parker went down prone behind the fire engine and looked under the vehicles to see if he could find Cory's feet. No; Cory wasn't in the immediate area of the fire engine, and farther away it was impossible to see anything.

He was getting back up on his feet when another set of headlights flashed on, farther to the left. He turned toward them, but almost instantly the lights switched off again, making the darkness darker than before.

So Cory hadn't known where Parker was, and now knew he had to be in here among the vehicles. Parker started toward where the headlights had flashed, and abruptly heard running.

The window in this pickup's driver's door was shut, but the door wasn't locked. Parker pulled it open, causing more light as the interior bulb went on, and switched on the headlights, to see Cory running as fast as he could toward the gate and the ramp. He dove around the far end of the Ford as Parker fired at him, just too late.

Parker slapped off these headlights, slammed the pickup door, and trotted after Cory, calling, "Tom! Get back!"

When he reached the gate, he stopped to listen. Not a sound from down there. Had Lindahl managed to get deeper into the clubhouse, locking doors after himself, or was Cory now moving around inside the building? Or was Cory waiting down there in the darkness for Parker to come after him?

Parker crouched low and slid over in front of the Ford, which would keep him invisible from down below. He waited, and still heard nothing, and gradually became aware that the darkness down there wasn't absolute. The lights were still on in the corridor beyond that room, and they gleamed a faint dark yellow through the thick glass of the small window in the door.

The gate was still slightly open, the way he'd left it. He sidled through, waited, inched forward. Infinitely slow, he traveled in a deep crouch down the ramp, left hand on the tilted concrete floor behind him, right hand holding the pistol out in front, eyes on that dim rectangle of light, hoping to see someone pass across in front of it.

As he advanced, he took shallow silent breaths through open mouth. He listened for any sound that would tell him where Cory was, but heard nothing.

At the bottom of the ramp, he stayed in the crouch, left hand now on the floor in front of himself. The duffel bag he'd brought in here from the safe room would be ahead and to his left; he moved toward it, always keeping his eye on that dim-lit window.

He had the bag. Turning slowly, bracing himself, he sat on it, knees wide, forearms on legs, hands and gun hanging downward. There was very little time to waste here, but there was time enough for this. He would wait, and Cory would reveal himself, and Parker would kill him. He would wait, and Lindahl would come back and make some sort of disturbance, flushing Cory out, and Parker would kill him.

The small rectangular amber gleam high up in the door was like a window in a castle far up a mountainside. Parker watched it, and breathed evenly, and permitted his body to relax, and waited.

six

"Ed! Ed! You down there?"

Maybe ten minutes had gone by, no more than that, the two of them silent in the dark, and all at once this urgent hushed call came down from the top of the ramp. Lindahl, not in the clubhouse, after all, but up there, outside, by the gate and the two cars.

Parker kept his eye on the yellow window in the door as he sat up straighter, gun hand now resting atop his right knee. If Lindahl was outside, he'd made his way all around to that other door, the one they'd come in. If he'd done that, wouldn't he have gone to look at the guards along the way, to see if they were alive or dead, and to take their guns? And if he'd done all that, he must not have left this room when Parker called the warning to him but earlier, the instant Parker had gone up the ramp and out of his sight. And he would have done that because he'd already had plans for the guards' guns.

Defensive plans, or a double cross?

"Ed! Where the hell are you?"

"Come down." It was Cory said that, from the other side of the black room, making his voice sound rough, indistinct.

But he hadn't sounded like Parker, because Lindahl up there at the top of the ramp said, with a quick quaver in his voice, "Who's that? Cory, is that you?"

There was a long pause, and then Cory called, in his own voice, "Yes. Come down."

Parker aimed at that sound, but it didn't go on long enough. If he couldn't be sure of his shot, he wouldn't take it.

Lindahl wasn't coming down. Instead, he was saying, "Where's Ed?"

"He killed my brother." Again too short to home in on.

"I know that," Lindahl said. "Did you kill him, Cory?"

Another long pause. "Yes."

"Cory, listen," Lindahl said. "You don't have any complaint against me, do you?"

"No."

"I didn't have anything to do with him and Cal. It made me sick when he told me about it."

No response from Cory; what response could he make?

Lindahl said, "Cory, come on, turn on the light down there, let's figure out what to do here."

"Where is it?"

"You see the window lit in the door there, to your left? It's just beyond that, on the left side of the door."

"Okay."

Parker raised the gun. Cory was now going to cross that light.

But Lindahl, up there at the top of the ramp, was at an angle to see first when Cory went by the door to block the window light for just an instant, so it was Lindahl who fired one of the guard's pistols. And missed.

Parker rolled to the floor on the far side of the duffel bag as Cory yelled and pulled open the door. He ran out of the room as Lindahl wasted two more shots from above.

There had been just that one instant of light when the door was open, and then dark again. Had Lindahl seen the shape of Parker, on the floor beyond the duffel bag, in that instant? Parker waited, listening, but didn't hear Lindahl coming down, so he got to his feet, crossed over to the door, and looked quickly out through that window to see only the empty corridor. Cory had run fast.

What would Cory do now? Most likely find a place where he could protect his back, hunker down, hope for an opportunity to get to Lindahl before Lindahl could get to him. And why had Lindahl taken those shots? Because he'd understood, just as Parker had, that Cory wanted revenge against both of them for the death of his brother.

So what was Lindahl doing now? Parker walked up the ramp, and at the top he could hear rustling sounds, out ahead. He moved along the side of the Ford and saw that the Jetta was rocking slightly. Lindahl was doing something inside there.

It took him a minute to figure out what had happened. Cory's first shot at Parker had smashed the rear side window of the Jetta on the driver's side. He had, of course, locked the car, but Lindahl had reached through the broken window to unlock that door. From outside, though, he couldn't reach far enough to unlock the driver's door, so he was now inside the Jetta, climbing over from the backseat to the front, grunting with the effort, clumsy in his haste.

Let them play it out. Lindahl was too busy with what he was doing to notice anything else, so Parker turned away, to stride by the clubhouse wall past that door they'd used for entry and along the wooden wall toward the parked vehicles. He stopped when he came to the first of them, a big boxy horse carrier.

By now, Lindahl was getting out of the Jetta, finished with whatever he'd needed to do in there. Cory would have the keys with him, so all Lindahl could have done was put the car in neutral.

Yes. Lindahl's Ford faced the gate and the ramp, its rear bumper against the rear bumper of the Jetta. Now Lindahl got behind the wheel of the Ford and backed it away from the gate, forcing the Jetta to roll forward. When he had the Jetta well out of his path, he looped around to back up against the gate and get out of the car.

Didn't he plan to do anything about Cory? Or had he understood he wouldn't be able to go back to his old life after this, so it wouldn't matter if somebody from those days wanted to kill him? Did he think the two duffel bags would give him a stronger chance at escape than just the one? Or did he believe Cory that Parker was dead, although Cory had only said so to try to bring Parker into the open, or to convince Lindahl that the shooting was over.

Lindahl got out of the Ford long enough to open the gates wide, then backed the car down the ramp and out of sight. An instant later the lights down there switched on, and an instant after that the near door opened and Cory stepped out.

seven

There wasn't much more light up here than before. It looked as though Lindahl had only switched on the deeper lights, the ones in the safe room. He must have been afraid to draw attention from the outside world. But there was enough added illumination to show Cory come out that door, gun in hand, and pause, first looking over toward that light, then looking at the parked vehicles instead.

Parker could hear Cory's thoughts as though he were saying them out loud. He wasn't sure if any of his bullets had hit Parker. Until he knew where Parker was, or where his body was, he didn't dare turn his back on anything. He knew he didn't have a lot of time before Lindahl would drive up out of there with the money, but first he had to account for Parker.

While Cory was working that out, standing in front of the still-open clubhouse door, as though he might reverse himself and go back inside again, Parker made his own move. The ambulance had ladder rungs bolted to its back, next to the door. Parker went up them and lay flat on the flat roof, facedown, head turned to watch Cory, who finally understood he'd have to come over here and search the vehicles for Parker, and that he'd better be both fast and careful.

All of which was making him nervous, taking some of the steel out of his rage. Down in the darkness, in the waiting time, Cory'd been as silent as Parker, or he wouldn't be alive now. But up here, as he moved in among the vehicles, he was gasping, quick rattle breaths that were like a road map showing his route through the dark.

The time for shooting Cory was gone, because the sound would set Lindahl off in some new scattered direction, and Parker wanted Lindahl, for the moment, just where he was. So he waited, lying on top of the ambulance, and below him Cory moved back and forth among the vehicles, looking inside, looking underneath, always with that gasping noise around him and that pistol hand stuck out front.

Parker waited, and the road map of breath-sounds turned the front of the ambulance, jittered down along its side, and Parker, pistol reversed, swung it down hard onto the back of that shaking head, driving Cory forward and facedown into the ground. He slammed to a stop down there like a broken film projector, frozen on that last frame.

Parker climbed down from the ambulance and didn't bother to check Cory's condition. If dead, he was dead. If alive he wouldn't be any use to anybody for a while.

When Parker reached the open gate at the top of the ramp, Lindahl was just stuffing the second of the duffel bags into the SUV, filling up the storage area behind the backseat. Parker left him to it and loped away to the outer gate in the surrounding wall, which they had left closed but not locked. He stepped through the opening as back there at the clubhouse bright headlights angled upward at the sky from below ground, then leveled out as the Ford appeared. The headlights disappeared for Parker as he moved to his right along the wooden wall.

Lindahl had to stop to open the gate, and when he did, Parker stepped forward into the headlights, saying, "You got our money."

Lindahl staggered. In grabbing the gate to try to brace himself, he made the gate swing instead, and nearly fell down. "Ed! For God's sake!"

Lindahl was not carrying a gun, so Parker put his in his pocket as he came around the end of the gate and said, "Help me carry my duffel out of there."

"Sure— You— He said you were dead."

"He was wrong. Come on, Tom, let's get this over with."

Parker opened the rear cargo door and looked in at the two long mounds, like body bags. Lindahl came and stood beside him, looking in at the bags. "I did it," he said, his voice quiet but proud. "I know, you and me together did it, but I did it. After all this time."

"We'll just put it on the ground outside," Parker said, reaching for the top duffel, "beside the wall."

"You don't want me to see your car."

"You don't need to see my car. Come on, Tom."

They put their arms around the end of the duffel and carried it around the car and through the gate and put it on the ground beside the wall. Looking down at it, Lindahl said, "Half the time, I was sure, if we ever got it, and I never thought we'd get it, but I was sure . . ." His voice trailed off, with a little vague hand gesture.

"You were sure I'd shoot you," Parker said. "I know."

"You could have, anytime."

Parker said, "You brought me the job, you went in on the job with me, that's yours."

Lindahl giggled; a strange sound out here. "You mean," he said, "like, honor among thieves?"

"No," Parker said. "I mean a professional is a professional. Take off, Tom, and stay away from roadblocks. That car might be burned by now."

"I'll be okay," Lindahl said. The giggle had opened some looseness inside him, some confidence, as though he'd suddenly had a drink. "So long," he said, and got behind the wheel of the Ford. His window was open; he looked out and might have said something else, but Parker shook his head, so Lindahl simply put the Ford in gear and drove away from there.

Once Lindahl had made the turn onto the dirt road leading to the county road, Parker went over to bring the Infiniti up close to the duffel. By then, Lindahl was out of sight. Parker wondered how far he'd get.